PASSAGE

A Time Travel Novel by

S. Mandel Joseph

ISBN: 9781655258763 (Paperback)

Library of Congress Control Number: 1-8181356341

Front cover image by Adrijus Guscia
Book design by www.rockingbookcovers.com.

Printed by KDP Publishing, Inc., in the United States of America.

First printing edition 2020.

"Choices create circumstances; decisions determine your future" – John Croyle

Prologue

1984: The murder.

I WAS IN A DREAM. And in that dream I was nineteen again, with my hair in a Ponytail with Scrunchies and shiny lip gloss saturating my lips. I was wearing ripped tights and a polished oversized shoulder padded blazer over a neon blouse.

I was standing in an empty parking lot near an abandoned building adjacent to a deserted playground filled with rusted memories of innocence.

Dead foliage and an eerie, purplish mist encircled the entire area.

The headlights of a vehicle appeared, cutting through the dense fog and coming to a stop in the parking lot, near the entrance to the dilapidated playground. I watched as it sat there, engine idling, waiting, headlights still on.

A few moments later, the dark silhouette of a man appeared wearing a hooded pullover and jogging pants. His outline was thick and husky and intimidating. His face hidden by the blackness of the night.

He kept his hands in the pockets of the pullover until he reached the vehicle. He looked around, checking the area, making sure no one else was around, before opening the door to the passenger side of the vehicle and getting in.

I strained my eyes to get a better look at him through the windshield. His face remained shadowed in darkness even as he pulled the hood down from his head.

He started talking to someone at the wheel of the car. At first, that person was shrouded in darkness until the dome light in the interior came on, and I saw that it was a woman.

Her face remained shadowed, but she had a fair skin tone with long, brownish blonde hair that covered her shoulders. Her frame was slender, but not fragile. She had a toned and wiry physique, athletic, though petite. Her nails were long and sharp and polished with colorful designs. She wore a gaudy jacket over a floral-pattern shirt to complete her flair.

I recognized the style she flaunted, the early eighties jewelry and chic that made people take a second glance if they saw her on the street. She had finesse, but with class. The man didn't. He seemed abrasive and brutish and rough-hewn as he lifted a beer to his mouth.

He reached over to kiss the woman, but she pushed him off of her. He didn't let that stop him from advancing. He forced himself on her, and she slapped him. He returned her blow with one of his own, striking her with a semi-circular punch to the head.

The sudden assault caught her off guard. She swayed, dazed and defenseless. She tried to get away from the man, but he grabbed her and shook her and began slapping her. She was screaming, bleeding, but he didn't care. He had become dark, driven by a sudden blind rage, hell-bent on hurting the woman and beating the life out of her.

He pulled a sharp, wood-handled knife from his pocket and jabbed the blade into the nape of her neck until the handle met the flesh.

The woman screamed.

That was when I ran to the vehicle, crying out, screaming to the top of my lungs, desperate to reach the woman.

My cries were mute to my ears, and no sound filled the night. No wind. No crickets. No air. Just a deafening silence. Until my scream reverberated throughout the parking lot, shattering the silence with a clap of thunder.

"*MOM!*"

That was when I saw the woman's face, etched in horror, dying. It was my mother. And she was reaching for me, even as the knife of the killer stabbed her in the back of her head.

As I raced toward the vehicle, moving in a haze of surrealism, the killer sprung from my mother's car and dashed toward the woods, dropping his beer. My screams stopped him in his tracks, and he turned, looking in my direction. But he did not see me. He seemed confused, at a loss, narrowing his eyes in a squinted gaze.

I caught a glimpse of his face. A face I would never forget—a face that would haunt me for the rest of my life. Those dark, soulless eyes piercing into mine, his jagged face covered by the unshaven growth of a scruffy, dirty beard. He grinned as he stood there, knowing he got away with murder.

He turned and ran into the woods, disappearing into the dense mist.

I moved faster toward the vehicle, reaching my arm out, screaming, the world around me moving in an illusory flow.

As I tried to reach my mother's car, I saw the death in her horrified gaze. I saw her take her last breath behind the wheel. Then I heard the echoing voice of a man.

"Anne!" his voice resonated in the night. "Anne, wake up! Wake up!"

I opened my eyes and realized I was standing on a balcony about to jump.

CHAPTER 1

Present Day.

I FELT THE HAND OF MY HUSBAND YANK ME from the balcony and pull me back into our bedroom.

"Anne! You're having another dream!" he shouted, hugging his arms around me, then grabbing me by my shoulders and shaking me. "Wake up! You're dreaming again."

For a moment, I remained in a daze until the real world began to materialize at the sound of his deep British pitch. I looked at him, my eyes glassy, as if I was coming out of a trance. "What? Tom…"

"You were screaming for your mother and started running to the balcony," he said. "It looked like you were about to jump."

When I realized what he said, and what I was about to do, I dropped to the floor, hugging myself, tearing. "Oh, my God. Oh, God. Tom…"

"Are you okay?" he asked, kneeling next to me.

"I'm sorry, Tom." I said, crying. "I'm sorry."

Tom caught his breath, looking toward the balcony, shaking his head. He was relieved, but upset. "Anne, you need to—"

"I know," I cut him off, knowing what he was going to say.

"It's getting worse, Anne," he said softly. "Psychiatry is not helping. Therapy isn't helping. You can't keep going on like this."

He squatted next to me, bringing his knees into his chest, sighing. "I wanna help you with this, but I'm out of options here," he said in exasperated breaths. "You've been seeing a psych for over three decades. You go to group therapy. I try my best to be there for you. But nothing seems to be helping."

My response came in guilty tears instead of words.

"I don't think you're ever going to move beyond this until you let go of the past," he said.

I shook my head. "I can't."

"You won't," he retorted. "You won't let go of your past. It's like you're choosing to live in misery."

"It's hard," I said to him, wiping the tears from my eyes.

"You're making it hard. Not just for yourself, but for those around you. We've been married for over two decades and in all of that time, you've never allowed yourself to get close to anyone except your therapist. You don't leave the house unless it's to visit your brother, visit your mother's grave or attend group therapy in that domestic violence program you run. That's it. You never go to the parks or theaters or out to dinner."

"I know."

"You don't have a real social life." His tone changed from sympathy to resentment. "This hasn't been easy for me, neither, Anne. There's nothing normal about what you're going through, and it's really draining the hell out of me."

He got up, running his hands through his graying strands of hair. He headed toward the bed and took deep breaths to calm himself. He looked at me, rubbing his hands together. "You know I love you, right?"

I nodded. "Yes. Of course."

"I want to continue helping you get through this," he said, softening his tone. "But I think we need some time apart."

Right away, I assumed it was another woman, looking at him through narrowing eyes.

"Who is she?" I asked.

He was caught off guard. "What? Who is who?"

"We've been married for how long now? Over twenty years, and now, all of a sudden, you want time apart. Seems damn suspicious to me, Tom. So who is she? Someone younger than you? There's an epidemic of older, rich men dating and marrying women half their age out there today."

He shook his head, sucking his teeth. "Stop being suspicious. That's not it at all. You're definitely barking up the wrong tree. Leaving you for another woman is the furthest thing from my mind.

That's not what this is about. This is about you letting go and moving on."

"We don't have to be apart for me to do that," I said to him.

"I know we don't. But sometimes I wonder if my being here hinders you."

"I wouldn't have made it this far in life if you hadn't been here for me, Tom. You've been my crutch, you've been my backbone, you've been everything. I can't make it through this without you. I need you, Tom. I need you and I still love you. You have to realize that."

"I do, Anne. I do. It's just hard for me sometimes. I'm doing this alone on my end. You have therapy."

"You're more than welcome to join us, you know."

He didn't find the offer humorous as he moved to sit next to me on the bed. "No thank you," he said.

I reached for his hand, and he took my hand in his, rubbing it gently.

"We don't talk about anything outside of domestic violence and what happened to your mother a long time ago," he finally said, his voice softer. "During the entire time we've been married, I've been more of a babysitter than a husband."

I looked up to the ceiling with a sigh. I hate that he felt that way, but I didn't have a retort. I knew it was better to remain silent and listen to him vent.

"I—I felt pity and sorrow and remorse for you when I first met you," he went on. "I felt bad for you because I couldn't imagine what you were going through. I felt I needed to be there for you, and I thought I could help you overcome your demons. But now—now I'm not sure anymore."

"You want a divorce?" I asked him.

He opened his mouth to speak, but nothing came out. He lowered his head, searching for an answer. He looked up at me, heaving a sigh. "I don't know," he said at first. Then, "No. No. I don't. I—I just want you to get better."

I got up and walked toward the bedroom door, opening it. I stopped to look back at him. "What if that doesn't happen?"

He looked at me with no response. I guess he didn't know what to say. He placed his hand over his face and rubbed his eyes. "Do you want to save our marriage?" he asked.

"You know the answer to that question," I replied. "You know how much I care for you… and love you. I survived so much of this because of you. But if I tell you, that after nearly thirty years, I can miraculously heal and move on, then that would be a lie. And that's the one thing this marriage has never been established on—lies."

With that, I left the room, closing the door, leaving him to consider his options.

CHAPTER TWO

November 1984.

ANDY STOOD ON THE COURTHOUSE STEPS, squeezing my hand tighter and tighter as the police appeared escorting my mother's killer from inside.

He came out holding his head down the moment the sunlight hit his face. A mob of reporters and angry spectators charged toward him, screaming obscenities and trying to get their hands on him.

His eyes never wandered in their direction or to ours, as he was led to a county police car, his hands cuffed in front of him. He wore a dingy denim shirt with soiled blue jeans that must have been stained from a scuffle with the police during his arrest. It was obvious he didn't surrender without a fight. He had bruises and cuts on his face and hands and his shirt was ripped along the sleeves.

His crimped threads of tousled dark hair flowed down to his shoulders and looked neglected. He lifted his head once, to waft the hair from his eyes.

That was when he looked toward me and Andy, a wild look in his inky, dark eyes, that sent chills through my body. He looked around at the cameras and the angry crowd gathered around him, displaying no guilt or remorse. He moved with indifference. He was as cold as a slab of concrete—the embodiment of a man walking in the biosphere of his own sinister evil.

Andy and I had arrived for his arraignment early that morning, but we never went into the courthouse. We waited outside, standing near my mother's sister, my Aunt Sharon, her husband, Uncle Owen, and several detectives.

Andy wore a cartoon T-shirt with shorts, and I had on a rad Schott Perfecto jacket with ripped jeans. My hair was a mess, and tears had ruined my eyeliner. The tears running down my cheek stopped when I saw the murderer. I frowned as I eyed him, visualizing myself spitting in his face. But before I got the chance to execute my vindictive fantasy, a gunshot rang out.

It detonated next to my ear with a thunderous explosion—sounding more like a canon than a gunshot and sending a throbbing chime through my eardrums.

I heard muffled screams over the ringing. People started screaming and running for cover.

My eyes dashed toward my mother's murderer, and I saw his eyes widen as he reached for his chest.

I saw the coaster-sized hole punctured center mass from what must have been the bullet. Blood poured from the wound, staining his shirt, as he collapsed into the arms of the police officers escorting him. One of them attended to him while the other one pointed in my direction.

Not at me, but someone next to me.

When I looked to my side, Andy was holding a revolver. It was the same gun my father had given to my mother after they separated. It was for protection, not murder. Somehow, Andy had found it and placed it into his school backpack. And he knew how to use it. Something he learned from our father during his first years of grammar school.

He held the gun steady, his brows knocked together in a fierce glare I had never seen before. He snarled in contempt with his lips curled in an icy hatred. At that moment, I was afraid of him.

My legs went numb and my upper body stiffened as I looked at him, catching my breath.

Two of the detectives near me wrestled the gun away from Andy and forced him to the ground, handcuffing him as he kicked and squirmed to get free.

The moment I saw them hurting my brother, I sprang into action, striking them across the back of their heads, struggling to reach Andy, but another detective grabbed me from behind and pulled me away.

Andy screamed and growled with a savage ferocity. For the first time since my mother's murder, I saw the stifled bitterness and rage erupt.

I cried out to him as the police dragged him toward a patrol car. He went into an animal craze, biting and spitting at the police as they placed him into the back seat of the car.

One officer got into the back seat with him, trying to restrain him. When they pulled off, Andy looked out the window, screaming for our mother.

I collapsed in the arms of the detective holding me, crying out for my brother, knowing, in my heart, I lost him as I had lost my mother.

And the man responsible for destroying my family gasped for air on the courthouse step, his chest heaving one final time before he died.

CHAPTER THREE

Present Day.

I SNAPPED BACK TO LIFE the moment I realized a car was blowing its horn behind me. I was stopped at a red light and didn't realize I had zoned out into a surreal recurrence of the day my brother murdered my mother's killer. I gathered myself as I looked into the rearview-mirror, and took my foot off the brake, driving off.

After an hour drive, I pulled up to the mental hospital my brother had been sent to years ago... around the time he reached adulthood.

I parked my luxury car in the usual parking space for visitors, and climbed out the car carrying the bag of goodies I brought along for Andy.

After going through a security checkpoint, I made my way into the building. I walked along several corridors until reaching my brother's room. Attendants guarded his door and stood in the hallway. When they saw me, they greeted me with nods and smiles, but I didn't return the friendly gestures. I kept my head down instead, and walked past them without a word. This was the last place I wanted to smile or be cordial. I hated coming here. I hated that my brother was here. It took everything in me not to break down into tears in front of them. But I held myself together as one of the attendants unlocked the door to Andy's room.

When I entered the small room, I saw my brother seated in a chair at the window—looking out, as usual. From the time when he woke up until it was time for him to sleep, that was where he stayed. Fourteen hours a day. He made no motions, no sound. He sat in the chair lifeless and distant, in a world far from this one.

He was thinner than usual. He had been refusing to eat his nurse had told me some weeks ago. The hospital had to force feed him three times a day. But he still enjoyed candy. There were candy wrappers on his unmade bed.

His hair had receded since the last time I saw him—which was three Fridays ago—and had started to gray. His face had become gaunt, but his boyish looks were still evident.

He wore a Charlie Brown T-shirt I had bought for him ten years ago. He loved Charlie Brown when he was young. Somewhere inside him, that child was still alive. I knew he was. Underneath the driveling, scrawny man who sat before me, Andy was in there.

He didn't acknowledge me as I entered the room. He never did. He never let anything or anyone distract him from the window. I walked over to the bed and emptied the bag of candy I was carrying.

All of his favorite candy bars as a kid spilled across it. I looked at him waiting for a reaction. He remained expressionless.

"It's me, Andy," I said. "I brought all your favorite yummies and goodies." I talked to him as if he was still that twelve-year-old boy I remembered before my mother's murder.

He stared out the window as if oblivious. I should have been used to his mental abandonment of this world by now, but I still found myself hopeful, waiting for a response. When one didn't come, I lowered my head, closing my eyes. I moved to the edge of his bed and looked around the room.

After a moment, I looked at him again, my eyes watering.

"I know I haven't been here to see you in a while," I said. "I'm sorry."

He remained motionless.

"Wanna know what I've been doing?" I knew he didn't, but I told him anyway. "I've been taking yoga classes. Between my group therapy sessions and self-defense training classes, and now yoga, I've been really busy. It takes my mind off of bad things."

He didn't blink or utter a sound.

I remained silent for a moment, looking around the room, unable to find the right words to get a response out of him.

I made my way to a framed photograph he had on a desk. It was a picture of him when he was twelve, hugging my mother on the last birthday we spent with her. I reached down and picked it up, staring at it for several moments. I placed it back on the desk and let out a long sigh.

"Andy? I know you're in there. I know you are. I know what happened to our mother took something away from you like it did to me. I remember how hurt and angry you were. I know that's why you did what you did."

I waited for a sign—any sign—that my words reached the brother buried deep inside the man sitting in that chair. But the Andy I knew, the baby brother I loved, had become an extinguished fire—an ash with no soul. I sighed again, raising my head, closing my eyes, letting the tears flow without wiping them away.

I knew he was somewhere in that body. I knew he heard my voice. I knew he knew who I was. And I knew I had to continue to try to find him and bring him back to the world of the living.

"I know you didn't mean to do it, Andy. You were only twelve years old. A young boy. You were scared and lonely and afraid and confused. And no one was there for you. I wish I would've been there for you."

He made a sudden gesture with his head, looking away from the window and down at his hands.

I moved closer to him. "You did what you did to a bad man. He deserved it. He deserved that bullet. He deserved to die. I wish I would've done it instead of you. I wish I could change places with you. I wish it would've been me. He took away our lives. He's the reason why you're here. I wish I could bring him back to life and kill him so you wouldn't have to."

Andy looked at me for a moment, his eyes lacking understanding.

I grabbed him and held him tight. "I love you, Andy. I love you with all my heart. I'm so sorry, baby brother. I am so sorry."

I kissed his forehead before walking to the bed and grabbing my purse.

"I'll be back to see you next Friday," I said. "I promise."

I allowed myself a slight smile before heading to the door and opening it. I stood in the doorway, looking back at him, waiting for him to motion, to utter a grunt, or show me some sign he heard every word I said. He never looked in my direction, and I knew I was expecting too much from him.

After all the years that had passed, I still wasn't used to seeing him in that state. And I still hoped he would one day snap out of it.

I turned away and walked into the hallway, closing the door to the room, holding my head down, avoiding eye contact with the attendants. I didn't want them to see my tears. I rushed toward an exit door to a staircase and raced down the steps. When I reached the lobby, I collapsed to the floor in a wail of emotion, allowing the inner pain to engulf me. The tears came fast and inexorable.

I thought, after all these years, I had grown beyond reacting to my brother's condition. But I hadn't. For the most part, I knew I wasn't crying because of his vegetated state. I cried because I knew he died the day Elroy Leonard took my mother away from him.

CHAPTER FOUR

AFTER LEAVING ANDY, I spent the next few hours in the gym. I had my own gym at home, but it wasn't the same as going to a venue where you gained motivation from the people around you.

My routine had been the same over the last twenty years: fifteen minutes of ab crunches, twenty minutes working the upper body muscles on a lat pull-down machine, ten minutes exercising my arms on cable bicep bars, fifteen minutes working my legs on a horizontal seated leg press, another twenty minutes on a cardio rowing machine and thirty-five minutes on a treadmill.

After sweating profusely, I made my way to the showers. I always spent twenty minutes or more washing myself and allowing the cascading water to cleanse my soul more than it did my body. Afterwards, I changed from my leggings and tank top to my karate uniform, and attended a forty-five minute kickboxing class adjacent to the gym. It was where I let off the most steam, and was able to take my mind off the past.

Two women from the domestic violence support group I founded twenty years ago trained alongside me, punching and kicking weight bags. One was Cheryl, in her late twenties, divorced, two kids, who had been a victim of domestic violence in her seven year marriage.

The other was Cynthia, in her mid thirties, also divorced, no children, but she came from a nine year long history of domestic violence from two marriages. She was a petite woman, introverted, timid, a bookworm, who wore glasses that amplified her eyes to the size of the thick lenses. She had been in the support group for six months, but made the maximum progress. Maybe it was because of her determination not to become a victim of abuse in the future.

They competed with me with every motion, every fierce movement, as I unleashed a full onslaught on the weight bags— punching, jabbing, striking and kicking it with every part of my body. But they had no idea what drove me, what kept me going, what made me violent, ferocious and relentless. And I never shared my inner motivation with them. I never talked about the strain my mother's murder had on my marriage or how my brother's mental condition wounded my soul. I showed them the tougher and formidable sinews of my stamina—a woman refusing to surrender to fatigue or pain. And that intimidated them as they stepped away from their weight bags and removed their gloves, standing there while watching me release my frustrations.

"You really put us younger women to shame, Anne," Cheryl joked.

I didn't allow her humor to break my concentration.

"I think you push yourself a little too hard," Cynthia added. "One of these days you're going to break something."

"Yeah, I just hope it's not a person," Cheryl chortled.

Our instructor, Akimitsu Yamamoto, a short man dressed in a red Keikogi, walked over and eyed me, shaking his head. When I felt him watching me, I stopped and caught my breath.

He walked with his hands behind his back, looking at the bruises on my legs and elbows.

"Why do you bring harm to your body?" he asked.

I tried to catch my breath to answer him. But before I could utter a word, he said, "Muay Thai, Tae Kwon Do and Gwon-gyokdo are all considered to be a form of defense, not attack. Your strength comes from the mind, not your body. You are using your body in anger... hatred... as if it was a weapon. I have seen you improve in form over the years, Anne, but not in values. Your concentration should always be on technique and inner self, not on the target. Kickboxing is more than a relief from stress or a simple workout. It is an art that requires discipline, not punishment."

With that, he bowed to Cheryl and Cynthia and walked away, leaving me to ponder his words.

I walked away from the gym removing my gloves and heading toward the locker room. Cheryl and Cynthia followed behind me. We were done for the day.

The support group meeting had been going on for an hour when I began addressing the seventeen women and four men who sat in a circle of chairs. We held the meeting twice a month at a local hotel auditorium. Mariana, a frumpish and a disheveled middle-aged woman, was the keynote speaker.

Mariana had been the voice of the group since I first founded it two decades ago, after divorcing her abusive husband. She sat in the circle of chairs next to me as I spoke.

"Dealing with the loss of someone you loved through violence is never easy," I said, holding the microphone close to my mouth. It was loud. I wanted everyone in the hotel to hear what I had to say. I felt a surge of passion in my speech.

"In fact, you never totally get over it," I went on. "The anger and the pain are hard to bury. So is the feeling of guilt. I was never a direct victim of domestic violence. Neither was my mother. She was murdered by a man who loved to drink and loved to cheat. But he had rejection issues—like many people do."

I stared at the men in the circle.

"After my mother ended their relationship, mainly because he was younger than her and immature, he kept begging for her to take him back. When she didn't, he murdered her. My mother never saw it coming. She didn't see him as a threat because she didn't believe a man would murder her for ending a relationship. She didn't think she was worth any man going through that. That's what she said to me. Those were her exact words, and I remember her saying them."

I looked at Cynthia as she wiped tears from her eyes.

"This man had stalked my mother for weeks after the relationship was over," I said. "He would show up at her job unannounced. He would threaten her over the phone. And she still didn't believe he would harm her."

At that moment, my voice cracked and I had to fight back tears.

"But you never know what a person is capable of when they're unstable. You never know the scars of that person's childhood or upbringing. You never know what could have happened in their life, making them a screwed up individual. You never know if they have no respect for women or if they even have respect for human life. This man had none. He took my mother's life without considering what it would do to me or my younger brother. What it would do to our entire family. All he thought about was what being rejected did to him."

I looked around the room. "There are others out there like him, some not even born yet—unstable, unsympathetic individuals who only care about themselves. People who react without considering consequences. And they're dangerous because you can't weed them out. You can't pick them out in a crowd."

I saw Mariana nod in agreement as she held Cynthia's hand.

"You never know when you meet somebody, if that person is going to kill you someday in a jealous rage or out of their unwillingness to let you go," I said. "This man refused to let my mother live because she refused to live with him as a part of her life. He couldn't just move on with his life and find someone else. Instead, he kept my mother from moving on with her own life by taking it from her."

I felt myself drifting into dark thoughts and distant memories as I rehashed the pain of the past and the man who had caused it.

"Elroy Leonard—that was his name—was an unhinged individual. And, unfortunately, there is an Elroy Leonard in every generation. Some of you may have dated one in your lifetime. Some of you may be married to one without even knowing it. In some cases there are warning signs, in others there are not. Some people pretend to be a certain way when you first meet them, then you discover a dark side—usually when it's too late. There are no manuals or support groups that can prevent anyone from becoming a victim of a crime of passion, domestic violence or jealousy. I've come to realize that in the many years I have been struggling with my mother's murder."

I looked toward Cynthia again, who agreed with me with a warm smile and a nod of the head.

"You just have to take the time to really get to know a person. You have to communicate with that person. Find out as much about them as you can. If that person comes from a dysfunctional family, or an abusive past, or doesn't respect their mother, or had an abusive father, or likes to hang around bad people, or abuses you emotionally or verbally, those are usually the telltale signs that you should abandon any chances of a relationship with that person."

I took a deep breath, looked toward the window, lowering my head. It took me a moment to get myself together and address the group again.

"If my mother had taken the time to know Elroy Leonard, and had more than a sexual relationship with him, it might have saved her life. But it didn't. So every month I hold these support groups in hopes that the messages will save yours. Or prevent sons and daughters from going through the hell my brother and I had to endure in our lifetime."

Everyone in the circle reacted to my pain with watery eyes and sighs. I went on, still fighting back the tears.

"They say no parent should have to bury a child. Well, no child should have to bury a parent from violence. What we are here today is a voice to reach those who don't realize they have one. To address a problem that has plagued women—and even some men—since humankind replenished this earth… violence against each other."

Everyone in the circle applauded, and their applauds resonated throughout the auditorium. I heard those applauds in my ears long after the meeting had ended. Afterwards, I said my farewells and made my way out of the hotel and to the parking lot. I climbed into my car, started it and sat in the seat a moment, clutching the steering wheel. When no one was around, I erupted into tears.

CHAPTER FIVE

LATER THAT DAY, after pulling myself together, I met with Susan Reardon, my psychiatrist, at her home office in Greenwich, Connecticut.

I started therapy with Susan soon after my mother's murder. I was nineteen about to turn twenty. We knew everything about each other, and kept no secrets from each other. It was Susan who introduced me to my husband, Tom, at a party, some years later.

She sat in her usual leather lounge chair, jotting down notes with her pencil and pad, and wearing her infamous Burberry eyeglasses and expensive Caviar Collection Fitted Boucle Jacket.

She was a few years older than me, but still had that same peachy blonde hair and bob cut she sported since her youthful thirties. She still had the same creamy smooth skin and wrinkle-free face she had when I first met her.

She had a large office with plush carpeting and fancy furniture. She kept water fountains and green, healthy plants on tables and along the window sills around the room. Nature-based artwork hung from the walls, and figurines of children were lined across her desk.

Since my first session, Susan's office had conveyed a sense of safety, healing and culture. She wanted her patients to feel as if they were in a sanctuary, where they felt comfortable discussing their problems and inner demons to a stranger.

She greeted me with her usual warm hug and kiss to the cheek, guiding me to the leather recliner where her patients spilled their guts.

As soon as I sat back in the recliner, Susan sat in her usual chair behind her desk, picking up a notepad and pencil.

"So," she started. "I'm assuming you went to see Andy today?"

"Yes," I responded.

"I can see it in your body language and eyes," she observed. "You feel drained?"

"Don't I always?" I responded with a grin.

"What happened?" she asked.

"The same. I blacked out at the wheel of my car again on my way to the hospital."

"For how long?" she asked, taking notes.

"I don't know," I said. "Sixty seconds. Maybe longer."

"Did you have the same dream?" she asked.

"Yes," I answered. "I always have the same dreams. Since my mother's murder I keep having them over and over again. I keep seeing her die. I keep seeing Andy killing the man who murdered her. I keep seeing my baby brother in an uncontrollable rage."

"What about the killer," she asked. "Are you seeing him clearer in each dream?"

"Just the ones with Andy," I replied. "But not when he murders my mother. It's funny how I can see him the day Andy shot him, but not when he murders my mother. He's always shrouded in mystery even though I know who he is. I would think his face would be clear in all my dreams."

I stopped and thought about it for a moment, looking at Susan.

"Do you think those dreams are trying to tell me something?" I asked her. "I mean, I've never seen or been to the crime scene where my mother died, but it's always so clear in my dreams. I can see every detail except the face of that bastard, Elroy Leonard."

"I don't think there are any sublime messages in your dreams, Anne," she responded. "I think you're wrestling with vulnerability." She paused, then added, "And a little guilt."

She waited for a response from me. I looked up at the ceiling, contemplating her words, trying to search my feelings to find any truth to her diagnosis.

"You wanted to be there for your mother, Anne," she went on. "You wanted to prevent her murder. You didn't like her boyfriend and you didn't trust him."

"No," I muttered in a whisper.

"You felt helpless that you couldn't be there to save or protect your mother," she said.

"I tried to warn her about him," I said, stiff across the recliner. "He was verbally abusive to my mother. He was younger than her. A smug bastard. He liked to drink and fight at bars. He was dangerous."

"I remember you telling me that you and your brother never took a liking to him."

"No, we didn't," I said. "He never interacted with me or Andy. He would come to the house at night, give my mother a good screw, then be gone before breakfast."

Susan hid her smile, remaining professional while scrawling notes on the paper. "What did you do to warn your mother?" she asked.

"I told her me and Andy didn't like him. I told her he was a bad influence for Andy—always drinking and cursing around my brother. He liked to brag about his military service, how he killed sand-people and towel-heads. He liked to brag about his sexual potency in front of me. A nineteen-year-old girl. I saw him as a pervert."

"How old was he at the time," Susan asked.

"In his thirties, maybe. I don't remember. My mother was in her forties when they met. He was eight years younger than her. Why is that important?"

"Because you called him a pervert," she responded.

"He was," I said adamantly.

"Did he ever try to come on to you?" she asked.

"Not directly," I told her. "But he would do stuff... like walking around and winking at me if I caught him in his underwear. Then sometimes he would talk about his sexual stamina when his friends were with him."

"Did he ever live at your house or just visit?" she asked.

"He would visit two to three times in a week," I said. "Spend nights, here and there. Sometimes he had his friends over watching sports with him. Then he started coming over less just before my mother ended the relationship. Those were happier times for me and Andy. The less we saw him, the better."

"Were you there when your mother ended the relationship with him?" she asked.

"No," I responded. "I was staying on campus. After she broke it off, Leonard would come around drunk yelling in front of the house, my brother told me. My mother had to call the cops on him several times. Then that bastard stopped coming to the house, but kept calling her. I thought he was gone and out of her life for good. Until that fateful night on Halloween. Before that, he would call her at work and beg for her to meet up with him after she got off. She kept refusing him. Then he started following her around, begging for her to take him back. And when she refused, he murdered her."

I didn't say another word, falling silent, dealing with my emotions. Tears began to trickle from my eyes. I turned my head to look toward the window, into the garden outside.

Susan allowed me a moment to reflect on my grief. She placed the pad and pencil on her desk, stood up, and walked over to me, taking my hand.

"I know it's hard, Anne," she said. "I know the memories are painful and—"

"—My mother didn't deserve to die like that."

"No woman does," Susan said. "Have you ever heard of femicide?"

I shook my head no.

"Femicide is homicide. It can be against women or, in some cases, men can be victims, too," she explained. "In seldom cases, though. It's mainly violence against women. Sometimes it's in the form of verbal harassment or emotional abuse, or it can be in the form of daily physical abuse." She paused, then added, "And even murder."

She walked around the room. "Men who commit femicide do so with every intention to harm or kill a woman. Femicide is different in the sense that it is usually always an act of homicide carried out by a husband or boyfriend or ex-partner. Someone the woman was intimate with."

"Why are you telling me this?" I asked.

"Statistics, Anne," she said. "Statistics. Thirty-five percent of all murders of women globally are reported to be committed by an intimate partner—a spouse or boyfriend. Those same statistics show that only five percent of murders of men are committed by a wife or girlfriend. And usually when they are, it's out of self-defense. That data alone should be enough to tell a woman that there's nothing wrong with her. There's something wrong with the men they chose to be intimate with. This is why you can't hold onto that guilt, Anne. Why you have to let go of the bitterness. It was nothing you did, nothing your mother did. And there was nothing, neither she nor you could have done to prevent the tragic circumstances that happened to her."

I looked away from her and toward the window again. I absorbed everything she said, but her words did little to provide comfort. My facial expression tightened into a frown that she noticed right away. The anger I felt came out in heavy breaths. I wanted to resign to her analysis, but didn't know how. Therapy hadn't changed the reality that my mother had been murdered and my brother lost. Nothing Susan said or suggested diminished the pain or the memories.

"You said everyone deals with pain and loss differently," I said. "I can't change or dissolve the way I deal with mine. I'm sorry, Susan, but I feel no different. I don't understand why. I can't understand why I can't let go or why I am still haunted by the memories. Maybe there is no clinical answers to my pain. Maybe the best therapy is talking about the therapy. Or maybe I'm just crazy."

"No, Anne," she said, "you're far from crazy. You loved your mother and she was taken from you in a horrible manner. Everyone deals with loss differently. It changes life in many ways. Yours changed. What happened to your mother scarred you. Left you bitter and weighed down by guilt. You wanted to do more to prevent your mother's murder and you feel responsible for your brother's actions."

I began wringing bumps on my hands and twitching my nose as I listened to Susan. It was difficult to digest what she was saying. I didn't want to hear it. I wanted a stiff drink. I wanted to forget the pain and bury the emotion. Even if it was temporary.

"I just wish I could trade places with Andy," I said. "I feel guilty about that. I wasn't there to help him deal with his own grief or anger. I was too wrapped up in my own. I feel like I could've prevented him from resorting to murder. Andy's not a killer. He was only twelve. He was just a baby. He didn't have anyone to lean on for support. Our father wasn't there. My mother's sister and her husband were dealing with the loss in their own way. They stayed with us, nurtured us, but they were in pain, too. It was so hard for all of us. Especially Andy."

"When did Andy first shut down?" she asked. She knew the answer to her question. It was a question she asked me during our first session over twenty years ago. But I think she was searching for a comprehensive answer.

I knew Susan. She didn't ask dumb questions and she had a flawless memory. If she was repeating herself, it was for a good reason.

"He became withdrawn soon after my mother was murdered," I responded. "He cried a lot on the day the police first came to our house and told us they had found my mother's body. The detectives told us she had expired. Andy went into a rage. He started fights at school. He stopped doing school work. He stopped watching television. But it wasn't until he killed Elroy Leonard, and got locked up in one of those juvenile detention centers, that he began to shut down completely. That's when he stopped talking. That's when he stopped being a child. He became an empty shell."

"That's why you feel guilty," Susan pointed out. "You saw the symptoms of his anger and depression before he murdered your mother's ex-boyfriend and you felt powerless to prevent it."

I didn't know what to say. Her analogy was on point. I knew she was right, but I never knew how to deal with it. I looked at her and nodded, wiping a tear I felt roll down my cheek.

"Anne—" She stopped herself, abruptly looking in the direction of the deluxe cherry wooden bar she had in the office. "You know I don't normally do this with my other patients, but you've always been an exception to the rule."

She walked to the bar and went behind the counter. She reached down, pulling out a bottle of Rose, Champagne and flaunting it as if she was holding a trophy.

She poured a glass for both of us. "I know you like the liquid medicine I prescribe."

She walked back to the recliner and handed me the drink. I took a sip and looked at her. "This is the best part of our session," I smirked.

"Cheers," she said, toasting her glass to thin air.

We forgot expensive wine was made to sip as we swallowed it from our glasses. At that moment, we said nothing to each other until we both finished enjoying the taste of the wine. When I finished my glass, she took it and walked back toward the bar, ready to pour a second glass, but she drifted into deep thought. I knew she had something she wanted to share with me, but she wasn't sure how to say it.

She looked back at me from the bar, tapping her finger against her wine glass while pursing her lips.

"Have you ever considered hypnotic treatment?" she said.

I was confused. "I'm not sure what that is."

"Hypnosis, Anne. Hypnotic therapy. Some call it hypnotherapy. It's a treatment some clinical specialist have used to treat anxiety, phobias, substance abuse and bad habits. I've seen where some clinical hypnotherapists have used it to successfully cure eating disorders, learning disorders, insomnia and relationship issues. I've even seen hypnotherapy help resolve medical conditions like digestive disorders, skin issues, and chemotherapy."

"And you really believe that stuff works?" I said with a sarcastic laugh.

"From a medical and psychological standpoint, yes. I've seen it have success on some of my own patients."

"I don't think my condition falls into the phobia or substance abuse category," I said, laughing it off and shaking my head.

"I know this hypnotherapist with a proven track record," she said. "He has a clinic here in New England, but a good drive away… in a secluded area. He's been treating people for nearly three decades. No malpractice suits. No complaints. He's a member of the Society for Clinical and Experimental Hypnosis with a doctorate level degree in medicine and psychology. He's a bit unique, though. Especially in his practice."

"Susan, you're not actually recommending I see a hypnotist, are you?" I blurted out.

"At this point, Anne, I'm willing to try anything to help you through this," she answered. "I haven't had success in the nearly three decades I've been treating you. And I've tried every technique and tool I've learned in the practice. It might be time for you to consider another clinical form of treatment. I believe this may be it."

I pondered on the thought for a moment, asking myself—if hypnosis would help. *Would this be the answer to my oppressive dreams and endless anguish?*

I knew in my heart that I wanted help. I also knew I needed help. But I had to be honest with myself and consider if being hypnotized would be that solution.

Putting myself aside, I thought about Tom and our marriage. I didn't want to lose him. I looked up at Susan and nodded. "Okay. If you really believe seeing this hypnotist would help…"

"I do." She walked over to her desk and reached into one of the drawers, pulling out a business card. She walked over to me and handed me the card. "This is his information. Please, Anne. Call him. Make an appointment. It won't hurt."

I looked over the business card.

"I wanted to recommend this treatment to you before. About three years ago."

"Why didn't you?"

"I wanted to wait."

"Wait for what?"

"To see if age would mend what therapy couldn't. Some healing takes time. That's why I haven't mentioned hypnosis as an alternative treatment."

I looked at the name on the business card. "Professor Singh," I muttered under my breath. I looked up at her. "Outside of his education, what else do you know about him?"

"I know he's expensive," she replied, going over to the bar and pouring another round of drinks for us.

"How expensive?" I asked.

"More expensive than building a bionic man," she said with a laugh.

"I'll talk to Tom tonight," I said.

"Do that." She came over and handed me my second glass of wine. "Anne, Professor Singh is no ordinary hypnotist."

"What do you mean?" I asked, sipping my wine.

"He has *special* abilities," she replied.

"Like what?"

"Like..." and she tilted her head as she uttered, "...maybe he would be best to answer that question when you meet with him."

"Okay," I agreed. "As long as I can feel comfortable with him, I have no problem looking into treatment."

"When you see what he has to offer, I think you'll feel more than comfortable with him. Like I said, he's unique."

With that, she gave me a sideways glance. She raised her glass to finish her wine. Afterwards, she looked at me, sighing, as if preparing herself for her next words.

"There is one other thing, Anne," she said, pondering on her words. "About Professor Singh."

"What is it?" I asked.

"There are different techniques to hypnotherapy," she said. "You don't want clinical or psychotherapeutic hypnosis. You want regression."

"What the hell is that?" I asked.

"I told you Professor Singh is unique. And so is his practice. They're more than just Hypnotherapists, Anne." Her eyes stared right into my soul as she spoke. "They have the ability to send you and your memories back in time."

CHAPTER SIX

I SAT IN THE LIVING ROOM LOOKING OUT THE WINDOW waiting for Tom to arrive home. He had called earlier to let me know he was going to be late. That was three hours ago, and it was now ten minutes after nine.

The deluge of rain pelting at the window had me worried. I saw the road that extended beyond the u-shaped driveway of the mansion. The dense fog was blanketed with a thickening dark fog, screening the trees in the distance and the boxed garden in the courtyard.

No thunder came with the torrent downpour. Instead, I listened to the steady rain beads knocking against the window panes and across the roof. Its cadence echoed throughout the entire mansion, drumming a tune that was almost therapeutic.

For a moment, I shut my eyes to listen. Rain often had that impression on me. Every beating drop was a piece of music that soothed the crux of my being. I felt as if I didn't have to be in the rain to let the moisture of its touch cleanse my skin.

When I opened my eyes, I saw the beam of light from my husband's Bentley Mulsanne shimmering through the heavy fog and rain. I took the old photograph I had of me, my mother and Andy in my lap, and set it back on the chaise. Then I walked from the living room to the foyer as my husband's car pulled up to the mansion.

I waited for him near the front door. After a moment, he rushed in, drenched from head to toe, shaking water from his umbrella. He pulled a newspaper from the inside of his rain jacket and took off his shoes.

"Hey," I said to him.

He glanced in my direction, but did not look at me. "Hello. You're still up. Thought you'd be asleep by now." His words were rushed. He wasn't happy to see me.

"I know. I waited for you."

"Why? What's wrong?" he asked, hanging up his rain jacket.

I didn't answer him. Instead, I walked over to him and took him by his hand, leading him into the living room, near the fireplace.

"I see you got the fire going," he said.

"Get cozy and dry yourself off," I responded. "Did you eat?"

"Not since lunch," he answered.

"I made dinner," I said.

"Thanks," he said. He looked at me, growing suspicious. Wondering why was I being nice to him?

"Okay, Anne…" he said. "What's going on? The fireplace? Dinner? What happened today?"

"I had a good session with Susan," I replied with a grin.

"That's good," he said, removing his suit jacket.

"It was the most enlightening session we ever had together," I told him.

He walked over to the bar to pour himself a drink.

"That's good," he said. "What was so different about today's session as opposed to the countless others you had with her?"

"A remedy," I said.

He gawked at me, holding his drink to his mouth, waiting for me to explain what I meant.

I walked over to him and handed him the business card Susan had given to me earlier. He looked it over.

"What's this?" he asked.

"A lifeline," I answered. It was the best word to describe the therapy.

He rubbed the nape of his neck, biting his lip. Then he looked at me through narrow eyes, skeptical.

"Susan says I should consider hypnosis as a treatment," I explained. "She believes it can work in my case."

He studied the business card. "So this professor—
Professor Singh—is a hypnotist?"

"Yes," I responded.

"And you believe this can work?"

"I believe I should give it a try," I said, walking toward the
sofa and sitting down.

Tom sat next to me.

"Hypnotherapy, huh?" He wanted to laugh, but held back. "I
don't know, Anne. Hypnotism seems more suggestive than
credible. I just don't see it as a sound medical treatment. Not like
psychotherapy."

"It's an alternative medical treatment," I said to him. "Susan
already made me aware of the risks. So did Professor Singh
himself."

"You spoke to him first?" He frowned. "You spoke to him
without coming to me?"

"Yes," I answered. "I was curious. Anxious. So I called him,
asked a few questions, and made the appointment to see him on
Monday. I know I should have spoken to you first, but, Tom, if it
works—if he can help me move forward, burying the past,
overcoming these feelings of regret, bitterness, anger, it's worth
it. It's worth living a normal life. It's worth saving our marriage."

He agreed with a nod.

"Our marriage is important to me, Tom," I said. "It always has been and always will be. You're all I have. That's worth the risk."

"So how does this work?" he asked. "They put you into a trance and you just forget your past and become a different person?"

He was being sarcastic, but I understood why. He didn't believe in anything non practical.

"You don't need any special preparation to undergo hypnosis," I said. "And it doesn't erase your memories or your soul. From what I know, you're still you, but without the pain or the hang-ups or the addictions. Whatever. I just believe it might work in my case. And so does Susan."

Tom considered the sincerity in my tone of voice.

"Okay," he said. "If you feel it will help, I'll support you any way I can. I'll pay whatever the cost is. When do you start treatment?"

"Monday," I answered.

"That soon? You know I leave for my business trip tomorrow. I won't be back until next week."

"I know, I know. I wasn't expecting you to be with me for the session. I can handle it by myself. I'll be okay."

He nodded his acceptance. However, it was a reluctant nod. I knew he wanted to be there with me. I knew he was concerned about my well-being. But I smiled, and kissed him, to reassure him that I would be fine.

"I love you, Tom, and I want to save our marriage. I want to be a better wife. I want to finally bury the pain and move on. This may be the only way."

He nodded again. "Okay. I'm here for you if you need me."

"I know you are," I smiled.

He turned away and walked toward the living room. For some reason, he stopped, lowering his head. After a moment, he raised his head again and looked at me.

"Anne. I know you want to get better. I know you want the best for us. And I'm happy to see you taking progressive steps. But hypnosis...? I may not be totally knowledgeable about the practice, but it seems a bit risky. You may not come out of it the same way you went in. So, just, please, be careful. These people mess with your memories."

I reassured him with a cheerful smile. "I'm sure I will be fine. I trust Susan."

He turned and made his way toward the living room. I heard him walk out to the foyer and up the stairs leading to our master bedroom. I looked around the living room, hugging myself, smiling. I stood up and walked over to the chaise where I placed the photograph of me, my mother and my brother. I picked it up and looked at it again.

At that moment, I knew what I was going to do. I knew I was going to make things better. I knew that, if the hypnosis worked, if my consciousness was sent back in time, I was going to go back and murder the man who killed my mother.

CHAPTER SEVEN

MONDAY CAME FAST. Tom had left for his business trip on Saturday, leaving me the check to pay for my first session—even though he had reservations. But that was my husband. Supportive.

I left the house at dawn, thinking about him as I drove nearly two hours to keep my appointment with Professor Singh.

Traffic was heavy and my GPS took me on the long, scenic route. But when I reached the building where Professor Singh had his practice, I grew apprehensive.

The building was hidden in a remote wooded area populated with thick trees. A checkpoint barrier with armed security met me at the gate. A security officer checked my I.D., called on his radio to verify my appointment, and pressed a button to lift the swing arm barrier, allowing me to drive through. I felt as if I was entering a top secret military base. I drove along a narrow, dirt path to the main building where two more armed security guards stood at the entrance.

One of them gestured for me to enter the parking garage of the building. As I drove near it, the metal roll up doors opened, and closed the moment I entered. I drove two levels down into another area where a fourth security guard greeted me. He waited for me to park my car, then he led me toward a door where we gained access from his I.D. badge.

Once I entered the main lobby, an attractive, young Indian woman greeted me with a smile.

"Good morning, Mrs. Weatherford," she said, her accent distinct and thick. "Welcome. Professor Singh is waiting for you on Level C. You can take the elevator over there to your right."

"Thank you," I said, making my way toward the elevator. When it arrived and I got on, the first thing I noticed was a control panel with floor number buttons. As I looked around, the elevator door closed shut. A robotic female voice spoke through the intercom.

"Level C," the voice said.

I arrived at Level C before I could inhale my next breath. When the doors opened, I walked into an octagonal receptionist station that was adjacent to a waiting area. Two women seated behind a reception desk greeted me with smiles. One of them looked up at me holding a clipboard.

"Good morning, ma'am," she said. "Professor Singh will be meeting with you in his private office. It's the second door to your right. Please go in and have a seat."

"Thank you."

I made my way to Professor Singh's office. Once inside, I sat in a chair facing his desk. I looked around and saw several degrees in frames hanging from the walls. He was educated in the United States and abroad. I counted at least five degrees.

Family photographs lined his desk. He had two children, a teenage boy and young daughter, wearing pattu langa clothing from their native land. His wife was Hindu, draped in a long skirt, a lehenga worn with choli and a dupatta scarf. Professor Singh wore a suit, no tie. He was a handsome man, maybe in his late forties or early fifties, with a graying beard. He appeared professional and refined.

I looked over to a shelf and saw statues of the Shiva god and Parvati and Durga and Lakshmi and Vishnu. I had spent time in India with Tom during one of his business trips and learned a great deal about the culture and religion. I recognized the statues and knew their origins. Except for one.

I walked toward it.

It was a female statue with black skin and a crown. She was naked with multiple arms, holding several different time pieces—a sundial, a mini clock tower, an incense clock, an hourglass, an astronomical clock, and early mechanical watches and equation clocks.

As I tilted my head to the side in curiosity, I noticed the realism of the statue's eyes, staring back at me as if it had a life of its own. A sudden fear raised the hairs on my arms and made me shiver.

I stepped back, moving away from the statue, but unable to break my gaze.

"Ah! Good morning!" a voice said from behind me.

It was Professor Singh. He entered his office jovial and upbeat, moving toward his desk, carrying a folder.

His sudden presence had snapped me out of my daze. I moved back to the chair at his desk and sat down.

"Sorry about that," I apologized to him.

"Sorry about what?" he asked.

"I was—I lost concentration," I stammered. I looked back at the statue. "I'm sorry, Professor, but that statue over there on your shelf…"

He looked in the direction I was pointing and realized I was indicating the statue.

"Oh, yes," he said, walking over toward it. He grabbed it from the shelf and held it up. "This is Kali. Kali is the Hindu goddess of death, time and doomsday. She is worshipped in Eastern and Southern India and specifically in Assam, Kerala,

Kashmir, Bengal. She is, like many Hindu deities, a multiple armed figure with the number of arms being four, eight, ten, twelve, or eighteen. Each arm usually holds an object—like a sword, or dagger, or trident, or drum, or chakra, or a whip, or a noose, or a shield. But here she bears the devices of time."

"Very unique," I said. "I know about some of the Hindu gods, but I've never seen that one before. Why is she holding mechanisms representing time? If you don't mind my asking?"

"Of course not," he replied. "She is the primary source of power for our shamans. She is an embodiment of time as well as death. She is the sole source of a kinetic timeline that transfers the essence and mind of an individual through time. I will explain more once we get the preliminaries taken care of. Is that fine with you?"

"Of course," I answered.

He placed the statue back on the shelf and walked back to his desk. He sat in a leather chair, opening the file he had with him when he entered the office. He looked through it as he addressed me.

"I received your medical records by fax from your doctor over the weekend," he said. "I also received Susan Reardon's prognosis and clinical evaluations. I have been friends with Mrs. Reardon for several years, so I know if she recommended you to us then she felt this process would be the only solution to your problem."

He closed the folder and set it back down on the desk. He looked at me, folding his hands together.

"Let's be clear about what it is we do here first," he said in a soft tone. "Is that fine with you?"

"Yes. Of course."

"Our practice is more than hypnosis," he said. "Yes, we treat patients through suggestive therapy and analysis, but we use hypnosis as a tool to connect to one's consciousness and memories. "

"You can see into a person's thoughts?" I asked.

"Not your thoughts, Mrs. Weatherford," he replied. "Your memories."

I grimaced in my chair. What he stated was hard to believe or digest.

He recognized my skepticism with a slight smile, leaning back in his chair. "Allow me to elaborate," he said. "Most hypnotherapy is commonly used along with other forms of psychological or medical treatment. Many healthcare professionals use the technique to treat anxiety, phobias, substance abuse and bad habits. There are many other applications hypnosis can be used for. Mainly psychological. For example, if you complain of headaches or back pains, hypnotherapy has proven successful in helping patients mentally deem that these discomforts do not exist."

"Sounds like miracle healing," I snipped.

Professor Singh gave a quaint smiled. "Not quite. Hypnotherapy does not require holy water or an audience."

"Susan said you can send a person's thoughts and feelings through time using hypnosis."

His face hardened. He stared at me several moments in silence, tapping his fingers against each other. It was as if I had told him his wife had cheated on him.

"That's what I paid for," I said.

He continued to tap his fingers against each other. He smiled, breaking the tension in the air, and leaned forward in his chair. "Yes," he said. "I saw the substantial amount you paid. And Susan did make me aware of your mental state. That is why I am here interviewing you. Not everyone is suited for hypnotic transference."

"Not everyone can afford to pay the millions my husband spent for hypnotherapy," I said with a sarcastic smirk. "I figure it must be an exclusive practice. Like this facility you have here. I've never been to a medical office hidden deep in the woods with private armed security everywhere."

He didn't give an answer. Instead, he smiled, and ignored my suggestive comment.

"You know what I need or I wouldn't be here. I read the forms you gave me to fill out. I signed the waivers. You are legally protected if anything goes wrong. So are you going to put me under or not?"

He leaned back in his chair again, hesitating. He scrutinized me, the way a cop would a suspect. This man had something to hide. I didn't know what or the why, but his expression told me he didn't want me asking too many questions.

He leaned forward in his chair again and dazzled me with his charming smile. "Hypnotic transference—or regression—is a portal, Mrs. Weatherford. It's a mental and physical and emotional passage through time. A person's attention is focused while in this state that everything happening around you is blocked out. In reality, the mind leaves the body, attaching itself to what was and what used to be."

"Sounds more mythological than religious. Even supernatural. Hard to believe. You do understand my cynicism, don't you?"

"Of course," he said, standing up. He started walking around the office. "When one visualizes time travel, they automatically see time machines or some physical means of transference through space and time. If you conceive time travel in a less physical sense and become amenable to the notion of transporting yourself through the metaphysical sphere of hypnotherapy, then your consciousness defies the physical principle of time travel and conducts your soul and essence through space and time."

He stopped near the Kali statue, taking it from the shelf again and looking at it.

"Kali is time," he said. "Kali is also death and doom. Kali channels her power into the mortal man to define time." He placed the statue back on the shelf and looked at me. "In our reality, that of human existence, one's consciousness does not have matter. Your consciousness does not adhere to the limitations of physical law. Your higher consciousness is what is left when the physical you is passed on."

He walked back over to the desk and crouched on the edge of it. "If you really want to open that passage through time, I really need to know why."

I fidgeted in my chair, slow to respond because I knew I had to choose my words carefully.

"Well, you read my file," I said. "You know I have been getting treatment since I was nineteen. It used to be daily up until my thirtieth birthday. Nothing helps. Not the therapy, the meds, the retreats, the wellness programs... nothing eases the trauma."

"I see," he said.

"In fact, it's been getting worse," I went on. "I keep having these recurring dreams of my mother's murder. They feel real. They feel like I'm actually there, going through it in real-time. I'm haunted by the memories of my brother killing the man who murdered my mother. I have this repressed guilt that I could have done more to stop my brother. To save him. I can't let go of what happened to him or what happened to my mother."

I stopped to look at him, expecting a reaction of sympathy. His expression was blank. Susan was a better listener.

"This trauma has been taking its toll on me and on my marriage," I told him. "I barely have sex with my husband, and, when we had sex, I was unable to produce a baby for him. He wants to adopt, but I'm too apprehensive to do that because I'm afraid to get attached, afraid to lose someone else."

"So you feel like reliving or experiencing those years would provide you with the inner peace you desire?" he asked.

"I don't know," I replied. "I hope so."

"Mrs. Weatherford, hypnotherapy comes with risks and adverse reactions," he pointed out. "You can end up with anxiety or false memories. You can become permanently trapped in hypnosis."

He got up and walked toward the other end of the office. "There are always precautions involved when a person experiences earlier events in their life. In no way can you amend or obstruct the past. You are only there as an observer, not a participant. If you so much as say or do anything that affects what has already been, you could become trapped in the past."

"I understand," I responded. "I am willing to accept those risks."

He turned to look at me, his eyes studying me. I knew he wanted to have no doubts that I would be clear on the dangers involved in time travel. My eyes pleaded with his for sympathy, for him to take the risk. I was ready to go under. At this point, I had to.

After a moment, he nodded and walked back over to his desk.

"Very well, then," he said. "Let's get started."

CHAPTER EIGHT

"I REALLY WANTED MY HUSBAND TO BE HERE before going under," I whined to a nurse as she strapped me into a powered electric bed.

I had been given a gown to wear over my under garments. Three female nurses surrounded me, attaching small, metal discs to my scalp that monitored the electrical activity of my brain. Neurological equipment was placed around me on nearby utility carts. Patient monitors, IV poles, computers and sophisticated medical equipment I had never seen before had been situated around the entire room.

As the nurses prodded me with needles and hard-wired me to machines, I looked at them and asked, "What are you doing?"

One of the nurses looked at me and smiled, "Please relax, Mrs. Weatherford. Everything will be okay."

I had no control over the tingling in my limbs and the tightening in my chest from the sudden anxiety flowing through my body. My heart palpitated with increased rapidity at the thought of going under hypnosis. I felt twisted knots in my stomach and my eyes darted around in my head. As my breathing accelerated, I had second thoughts that caused my upper body to jolt violently. The nurse grabbed my shoulders and held me in place.

"Do not worry, Mrs. Weatherford, " I heard Professor Singh say from behind me. "We are merely monitoring your vitals and brain function."

I smiled as he walked around to the side of the electric bed. "I imagined myself stretched out on a sofa, fully clothed, with a hypnotist standing over me, rubbing my temples gently, and putting me into a trance. I had no idea I was going to be surgically implanted into HAL 9000."

He chuckled. "Ah, yes, I remember that movie. It was an American classic."

He walked around the room, checking the machines and instruments. "Hypnotherapy is an intricate and delicate treatment, Mrs. Weahterford. Especially when it involves the application of regression and thought transference. The side effects can cause anxiety or distress, or spontaneous impulses that could not only damage the patient's mind, but their body as well."

"Has that ever happened?" I asked.

"We have precautions," he answered. "That's what you see here. The transference of the mind and consciousness needs to be monitored as the patient's memories relive the past."

"So, in my mind, I will actually be there? Back in 1984? Back in my teenage self?"

"Absolutely," he responded with a grin.

"How does that work?" I asked. "What happens to the younger me? Where does she go?"

"Your current memories and essence neutralizes your younger self," he explained. "Your younger consciousness is immobilized, so to speak. The spirit and mind of the same person cannot exist at the same time in the same body. The body is just a shell that accommodates the mind and the soul. When that body is overtaken by the metaphysics of a being, it becomes a host to that consciousness."

He stood over me, looking down at me. His look told me without words that what I was getting into was dangerous. He wanted to make sure I was clear on that.

I gave him a nod, and he nodded back. We understood each other. There was no turning back.

"Are you relaxed?" he asked.

I nodded yes. He smiled and placed his fingers gently against my temples.

"You seem anxious," he said.

"I'm looking forward to going back," I said. "I had a great figure at nineteen."

My remark brought a brief smirk to his face. It didn't last. His expression became solemn and intense. "Through your memories, your passage through time will begin at the exact age and place and year you end your journey. Once your consciousness and essence are there, you will have eight hours to relive your past."

"Why only eight hours?" I asked.

"It can be eight hours or twenty-four hours. I can transfer your consciousness for a moment or a day. I have found, during my practice, the less time you spend reliving the past, the better. Sometimes, any time over an hour poses a grave threat to the person's subconsciousness. They can become lost in their past memories. We try to keep the hypnosis to a minimum of four hours. For you, we made an exception."

"I thought it would be longer than that. What if I need more time there?"

"More time for what?"

"To enjoy the memories," I responded.

"Maybe I didn't explain thoroughly how this works, Mrs. Weatherford," he said, removing his fingers from my pulsating temple. "It is through deep meditative techniques, and through hypnosis that opens the passageway allowing you to travel back through time to heal yourself. This is not done through physical interaction with your past."

He looked at me, straight into my eyes, making sure I got the message.

"The hypnosis technique allows you to console and comfort yourself during your experience of something dismal or traumatic that happened to you in that time." He said. "You cannot—and must not— change the ordeal or circumstance that caused the trauma. You can only see it and nurse it. Through emotions and your mind. Not through verbal or physical contact."

"I understand," I said, half listening.

"In order for you to understand what regression and transference through time is," he said, "look at it as if you were watching yourself on television. You see your past acted out on the screen, but you can only observe it. You cannot modify it. You cannot reach into the television and disrupt the performance as it occurs. The show is already scripted and any interference can change the ending in an adverse way."

"I understand."

"I can only transmit your thoughts and memories through time for a short duration," he added. "I know many people would like to spend days and even weeks reliving their past, but it's a draining process. For eight hours, my job is to keep you in a trance, channeling the quantum physics of space and time. That's eight hours without rest. That is why this treatment has limits. Not just to the amount of time you get to spend in the past, but how many times you are allowed therapy. I can only send a patient back once. That's it. Never more than that."

"Why is that?" I asked.

"Imagine a person going back through time and seeing something that they may be able to change or do over again. They see this as their one chance to make things better for themselves. If they miss that opportunity during their first hypnotic treatment, they will use a second session to make the correction that they missed during the first treatment."

He stood behind me and touched my temples with his fingers. I felt a sudden shudder through my body. I felt my mind muddling. With one touch, whatever powers he possessed, was now making a connection to my inner thoughts.

"Time travel is dangerous, Mrs. Weatherford," he continued. "Especially through physical interference. There is no safe way to go back and repair something broken in your past. You are only there as an observer... a visitor."

"What if I get back there and forget something I said or did during that time?" I asked. "What if I can't remember anything pertinent?"

"In the past, you will be nothing more than a ghost," he answered. "An astral essence in a time and place existing only in memory. As real as everything around you will seem, it's only a visual replay of your consciousness. Now relax. Close your eyes. Open your mind to me."

His voice had faded into a soothing whisper that I heard in my mind. I was still conscious of my present reality, but I began to feel my mind—and even my soul—drift into an out-of-body experience.

"Visualize yourself in that exact moment that you want to travel back in time to and allow the feeling of that moment to bring you back to the time it first started."

His voice became an echo in my mind, reiterating the words: "Relax... relax... relax..."

And—with the snap of a finger—I went into a trance. I no longer felt the electric bed I had been strapped to. I no longer felt weight or motion. I felt my consciousness moving, my soul pulling away from my body. I felt a sense of buoyancy, a sensation of relief as my mind drifted through space and time.

I traveled through a never ending void of darkness that stretched to an eternity. I saw my essence and consciousness flowing through a vortex of exploding stars and particles. Cosmic clouds engulfed my mind, and I stood alone, in a dimensional space filled with streaming lights and gray clouds.

It felt as if I was in an ethereal state, in a dream similar to the one of my mother's murder.

A smothering fog obscured the world's sights from my mind's eye. I heard the professor's voice in my head telling me to relax. With each light step my consciousness took, I perceived his voice dwindling into whispers. Until… it wasn't there in my head anymore.

I felt an otherworldly sensation encompass the world I was in. I felt misplaced, as if I had been dropped off in the middle of nowhere.

I began to feel the tangible ambiances of the world around me. I felt the pavement of a sidewalk, and looked down at my feet to see concrete—a sidewalk, as it became visible from the dispelling mist. I saw the shoes I was wearing: Vince Camuto women's Helayn blue Gladiator sandal shoes. An 80s fashion trend.

I wore the same padded shoulder blazer from my dreams with pin-striped jeans tight around my waist and thighs. I felt the weight of drop dangle earrings in my ears and makeup smeared across my face.

I looked up and began to see children running through the fog as it continued to dissipate. The children were wearing costumes and carrying orange jack-o'-lantern treat buckets. They ran through the street and toward homes, shouting, "Trick or treat!"

One of them ran into me, and I *felt* the impact of her body slamming into mine. As she ran off, I began to see the neighborhood through the thinning haze.

Modest Victorian homes along a tree lined street of colorful autumn leaves. Dim streetlights that cast shadows across the dark asphalt. Cars in every driveway. I knew the Midwestern ambiance surrounding me. I knew it well. I grew up here.

I made it into my past.

CHAPTER NINE

THE MOMENT I SAW MY OLD HOUSE, my heart accelerated.

It looked brand-new. The way I had remembered it. Bright. Simple. Traditional. A Folk Victorian style home inviting you into its modesty and charm.

I became flooded with adolescent memories as I moved toward it, excited by the thought of its refuge and solace. But each step was slow. Everything around me seemed surreal. The world moved in slow motion. I felt as if I was moving through a cloud, spirited into the air.

I felt the frigid evening breeze rush through the fabric of my clothes and the cold concrete penetrate the soles of my shoes.

The late October frost was normal for this time of the year, and had begun to water my eyes and redden my nose. The aroma of pumpkins on porches with burning candles inside of them triggered my senses as the scent permeated the neighborhood.

Candy wrappers blew over the leaf-strewn sidewalks on both sides of the street, and the muffled sounds of Halloween revelries resonated from homes. Neighbors dressed to trick or treat stepped out onto their porches to dispense candy and money into the hands and bright orange jack-o'-lantern buckets of children. Even the teenagers cashed in on the traditional celebration, donning scary costumes and carrying paper bags.

I knew many of them. They were my friends. I went to school with them. Partied with them. Ate in their homes. And dated a few of the promiscuous males I thought were cute at the time.

I wanted to reach out to them, touch them, make sure I was real to them. But my feet kept moving in the direction of my old house, where the curtains were drawn back, and inside grownups in costumes were moving around and celebrating.

We celebrated the tradition every year with spooky decorations: cutout skeletons and cardstock pumpkins taped to the front door, a vintage Dracula and coffin beside a hand-cut ghost on the front lawn, flickering orange lights wrapped around the front porch and wooden fence.

In each window, a jack-o'-lantern, with their eyes and mouths carved out and burning lights glimmering from inside, decorated the sills. I remembered each one. Every Halloween I gutted them with my mother and brother.

This had to be real. It didn't feel like a dream. I felt the brisk air and smelled the aroma of the pumpkins. *It had to be real!*

But no trick or treating child who shot past me acknowledged me. No masked face in the crowd of teens called out to me in recognition. It was as if I wasn't there.

I walked up to the front of my old house, looking around at the decorations, touching the ones I had placed on the door myself in the Halloween of 1984.

They were tangible.

I opened the door and walked into the house, remembering this night as I walked from the foyer to the living room.

People partied in the living room, dressed in costumes, each holding a glass of orange-colored drinks. They filled the living room with conversation and laughter. Some of them were neighbors, but many of them were my mother's friends and co-workers. They loved celebrating Halloween with her, at our house. This was to be their last year celebrating together.

They didn't notice me as I sauntered past them, heading upstairs to the second floor. I dragged my hands along the railing and walls as I went. I wanted to feel the authenticity of the house. I wanted to cherish it. This had been my home for nineteen years—a lifetime to me. And every moment I had spent here had been in bliss—until the night my mother was murdered—this night.

Once I reached the top of the stairs, I headed straight to my old bedroom. The door was closed to keep Andy out. I walked up to it and placed my palm against the solid wood. I felt the grain against my skin, and it felt real.

I turned the knob with slow caution and walked inside.

It felt small as I walked from one corner to the next, gawking at the Michael Jackson and Adam Ant posters on the walls. For nearly two decades I lived in a mansion. My powder room was three times the size of my teenage bedroom.

But as I walked around, I mused mover over the memories than the size. Every square inch of the room's décor was filled with the glow of the teenager I once was—from the pastel wall colors and pink bed valance, to the white desk with my awkward Apple computer that sat on it.

On my bed, there were stuffed animals sprawled across the pillows. I reached for one, picking it up and sniffing its fake fur. All of it conveyed remembrances of an innocence forgotten through time.

I spent several moments in a daze as I explored the bedroom. I came to the drawer of the night table near my old bed and opened it, pulling out my old diary. I rubbed my fingers across the front cover, then opened the first page, skimming through it. I wanted to recall what I was thinking and what I was feeling as a teenage girl. I wanted to remember the good place I was in before the murder.

As I read through the diary, I heard the scream of a boy. I looked to see Andy darting through the hallway past my bedroom door. I rushed out into the hallway and watched him race down the stairs. He was dressed as a ghost.

"Andy…"

He did not answer.

I heard another sound. A woman's voice singing. I turned around and saw my mother walking from her bedroom and into the bathroom.

"Mom…?"

The shock of seeing her alive immobilized my entire body. I swallowed a lump in my throat before rallying the nerve to move my legs to the bathroom. When I reached the door, I looked inside and saw her, putting on makeup, adjusting her outfit. She was wearing the same outfit I saw in my dreams the night of her murder.

My mouth fell open, but no words came out. My eyes bulged from their sockets and I felt my heart thumping as I watched her inspecting her clothes in the mirror. She was humming a tune to one of her favorite songs, smiling and happy, as I remembered her.

She was about to turn and head out the door when she saw me standing there.

She grabbed at her top, startled.

"Oh, my god. You scared me. How long have you been standing there?"

I looked at her, agape. "You can… see me?"

"Of course I can see you," she answered. "You're standing in my way. Now move."

She walked past me and headed back toward her bedroom.

"How long have you been home?" she asked me. "I've been waiting for you. You must've taken the bus. I told you to take a cab from the campus. It's faster, darling."

I walked toward her bedroom and watched her as she moved around, grabbing makeup, money, jewelry from tables and dressers around the room and placing them into her handbag.

"Where the hell are my house keys?" she asked herself. She started looking around the room for her keys. "Help me find my house keys, sweetie."

I walked into the room still unable to utter a single word.

"Everyone is getting ready to head over to Eddie and Myrna's for the costume party." she said to me. "I have to head over to your aunt Sharon's first, so I need you to take your brother trick or treating."

I shuddered, remembering that when she leaves, I would never see her again.

"You can't go," I said under my breath.

She stopped and looked at me. "What?"

"You can't go!" I yelled.

"And why not?" she asked.

Should I tell her? Should I come right out and change the events of *time*? I didn't know what to do. I hesitated, stammered. "Andy needs you," I said.

"You can watch Andy," she replied as she headed toward her closet and began digging through the pockets of her clothes. "I'll only be gone for a few hours."

"No you won't!" I shouted.

"My keys have to be here somewhere," she said to herself, ignoring my pleas.

I flourished my frustration through jerky motions and rushed speech. "Mom, you can't go. You have to stay home."

"Here they are!" she said with excitement, as she found her keys. She rushed over to grab her handbag, looking back at me. "Now why on earth would I have to stay home? You know I celebrate Halloween with friends and family every year. This is nothing new."

"Where's Elroy?" I asked her.

"Elroy won't be there," she replied. "Elroy is not a part of my life anymore, little darling. And why is that any of your business?"

"Mom, you can't go," I pleaded. "Elroy is a murderer, mom! He's—"

"A murderer?" she laughed. "Elroy is many things, sweetie, but a murderer he is not. I know you and your brother don't like him, but he's never coming around here again. It's over between me and him. Finito!"

She grabbed her bag and rushed out the room. I chased after her.

"Mom, please, you have to listen to me!"

"I will call you later after I pick up my costume at your aunt's and get over to Eddie and Myrna's house."

"You never make it to their house!" I shouted.

She wouldn't listen. She rushed down the steps and out the house, making her way toward the driveway where her blue Chevy Caprice was parked.

"Mom! Would you listen! Please! Your life depends on it! Please don't go! Stay, mom! Stay for Andy! We need you, mom! We need you! Mom, please!"

She got into her car, ignoring my plea.

"I don't know what's gotten into you, Anne," she said as she searched her bag for eyeliner. "Ever since you've gone off to college, you come back home acting strange. I really hope it's not a boy. Or drugs."

"Mom, I need for you to believe me," I begged her. "I need you to listen to me. Whatever you do, don't meet up with Elroy Leonard tonight. He's going to---he's going to—"

She waited for me to spit it out. "He's going to what, Anne?"

I lowered my head, unable to tell her. *What was I supposed to say?* I'm not the Anne you know. I'm really your daughter from the future in this teenage body. I hesitated to answer her, and she sighed.

"Listen, Anne, I'll be home before midnight, okay? You can talk to me about whatever your issues are later. Okay? And stop getting yourself upset over something that doesn't concern you." With that, she put the keys in the ignition and started the car.

"Mom... I love you," I uttered softly, my eyes tearing. "I won't let you die again. I can't. "

"What are you talking about? No one is dying, Anne. Now would you go back in the house and take your brother trick or treating!"

I held on to the door of the car crying. "I can't let you go, mom. Elroy Leonard is going to—I think he's going to harm you, mom!"

She frowned, shaking her head, growing impatient. "Okay, that's enough, Anne! You hear me? Stop that! No man is going to hurt me! You got that? I'm fine! Now, stop that crying and go do what I asked! I'll be back soon. I have to go. Okay? I have to go."

She put her foot on the gas and the car pulled out of the driveway, causing me to lose my grip on the door.

I charged after her.

"Mom! Mom, come back!"

She drove up the street, ignoring me, disappearing around the corner. I ran as fast as I could to keep up. My legs in my teenage body had the stamina and speed my future body did not. But when I reached the end of the street, I didn't see her car. She had already driven on to the next block. There was no way I could catch up to her now. I stopped and caught my breath, considering my next option. I turned and ran back to the house. I wasn't going to let her die again.

One of my neighbors, who was standing on his porch dispensing candy to the kids trick-or-treating, saw me and shouted, "Anne! Anne, what's wrong?"

I had no time to stop and answer him. My mother was about to be murdered again, and I had to stop that from happening. I had to intervene, no matter what it did to the timeline.

I dashed through the front yard and into the house, racing from the living room to the kitchen, looking for Andy.

"Andy!" I yelled. "Where are you? Andy!"

"Are we going trick-or-treating now?" I heard him ask from behind me.

I turned and saw him standing in the entrance to the kitchen, still wearing his ghost costume and holding his jack-o'-lantern bucket.

I grabbed him by the shoulders. Then I hugged him and kissed his hooded face.

"Andy, I need you to listen to me. Mom's in trouble, Andy."

"What kind of trouble?"

"That man! Her boyfriend! That fucker we hate! He's going to hurt mom. I need to stop him! I need to know where mom put the gun daddy gave to her for protection."

He hesitated to answer me, scared. "I—I don't know."

"Andy, I know you know where it is. You're not going to get in trouble for telling me. Mom needs me right now. She's in trouble. Where's the gun?"

"She hid it," he said with his head down.

"Where, Andy? Where did she hide it?"

"Upstairs," he said, his voice shaking. "In her closet. In a gray shoe box."

I raced from the kitchen.

"I wasn't going to touch it!" Andy shouted after me.

Little did he know, he was. But I didn't have time to tell him that.

I had one thought: save my mother's life.

In a panic, I hurried to her bedroom and to her closet. I began rummaging through it, tossing shoeboxes and clothes from it until I saw the gray shoebox.

I grabbed it and placed it on my mother's bed, opening it.

Sure enough, there it was—the .44 Magnum Andy used to kill Elroy Leonard—Its polished silver barrel as clean as a brand-new nickel. They dubbed it the Astra Terminator, a compact version of the large-frame .44 Magnum pistol. Made for one thing: killing another human being. And that was what I intended to do with it.

CHAPTER TEN

I TOOK THE GUN FROM THE SHOE BOX and stuffed it down my jeans, tucking my blouse over it to cover the black rubber handle. I rushed from the bedroom and headed downstairs.

Andy was standing in the foyer, still waiting to go trick-or-treating. I saw the disappointment in his eyes through the cut-out eye slits made in his ghost costume. I walked over to him, lifted the hood to his ghost costume, and kissed him on the forehead.

"I love you, Andy," I said.

I turned and rushed out the front door, cutting across the lawn.

Andy stood in the front doorway removing the hood from his costume.

"I still want to go trick-or-treating!" he yelled after me.

"Stay in the house until I get back," I said as I hurried up the street. "Lock the doors."

Andy, pouting, walked back into the house and slammed the door shut.

I wished I had the time to make him understand what was happening, but time was running out for my mother. I had to hurry. I rushed toward the home of one of my neighborhoods. I needed a car, and I knew he would be the sole person I could depend on for that.

I ran up to the door of his house and rang the doorbell. I waited a moment, then knocked. After a few moments, he answered the door.

Steve Mitchell, the nerdiest guy in the neighborhood.

He stood behind his screen door chewing on candy that was supposed to be for the children trick-or-treating.

He looked surprised to see me, but curious at the same time. "Hey, Anne," he said. He opened the screen door and walked out onto the porch. "What's up?"

"I need your help, Steve," I said.

"What do you need?" he asked.

"Your car."

"You're kidding, right? You know that car doesn't leave that driveway without its owner."

"I'll pay you."

"You don't even have insurance. Sorry, not gonna happen."

"Steve, I really need your help."

"You didn't tell me why."

"My mother. She's in danger."

"Danger? What happened?"

"I don't have time to explain, Steve. She's running out of time and so am I."

"So why don't you call the police?"

"The police are for when *after* the crime happens. Come on, Steve."

"I can't. That car's my most valuable possession. It's a chick magnet."

I gave him a look. He was no ladies man. He was a dork with pimples.

"Then I'll pay you to drive me."

I had his interest.

"How much?"

"Eighty now. Two hundred when you get me there and back."

He thought about it.

I pulled him by his plaid shirt and stuffed the eighty dollars in the right pocket, dragging him from the porch at the same time.

"Hey, wait a minute!" he shouted. "I'm house-sitting until my folks get home."

"I'll get you back home in time," I said as I pulled him from the porch to his driveway where an all-black Ford Mustang SVO was parked next to a Buick station wagon.

"Do you have the keys?" I asked him.

He dug into his pants pocket and pulled out the keys to the Mustang.

"Got 'em right here," he said.

"Get in," I ordered him.

"Where exactly are we going?" he asked me as he opened the passenger side door. I climbed in without a word. He rushed around to the driver's side and unlocked the door, getting in.

He put the key in the ignition, hesitating. I heard him breathing heavy and felt his eyes narrowing in on my teenage breasts.

"Is this a bad time to tell you I have a crush on you?"

I looked at him. "Really, Steve? Now is not the time."

"Okay, I just wanted to put that out there," he said, starting the car.

"Steve, I'm old enough to be your mother."

He looked at me, making a face. "What?"

"Never mind. Just drive."

The engine roared, and he backed out the driveway, tires squealing, smoking the pavement.

He threw the car in drive and raced up the street.

I put on my seat belt and reached into my jeans, pulling out the gun.

His eyes widened when he saw it. "What the hell is that for?"

"Not what. Who."

He put his foot on the brake, slowing down. "Whoa, wait, hold up. Is that thing loaded? Are you going to use that on somebody? I can't drive chicks around who carry around bigger guns than Dirty Harry. This is not cool, Anne. It's not cool."

"Steve, it's all right," I said. "It's my dad's gun. He left it with us after divorcing my mother. He wanted us to have protection. And it's smaller than Dirty Harry's gun."

"What do you need that thing for? We're in a good neighborhood!" he said. "Nothing bad ever happens around here."

"That's going to change after tonight," I said.

He looked at me, shaking his head. "Oh, man. I wish I would've known you had issues before I let you in my car."

I sighed. I had to tell him something. Maybe the truth would work. "Okay, Steve, I'm going to tell you this only because I know you won't believe me and therefore won't repeat it."

"Please, tell me something," he said. "I'm hyperventilating here."

"I'm not the Anne you grew up with and know from the neighborhood," I explained.

He made a face. "What're you then? A body snatcher?"

"No, Steve. I'm still Anne. But a little older. Thirty-six years older."

"What?"

"I know. I still look like the Anne you know. Young and stunning. But that's only on the outside. Inside, I'm an aging woman in her mid fifties with knee problems and an addiction to Merlot wine."

He looked at me with his mouth open. He shook his head in disbelief.

"Don't believe me, do you?" I said with a grin.

"Uh, no, not really. For all I know this can be a trick you and your sorority sisters are playing on me. Or you're high off some new college drugs I have yet to experience. Or maybe, just maybe, you found a creative way of expressing your female power of rejection."

"In my time, Steve, I spent several years learning self-defense and marksmanship. It helped me through some difficult times. It gave me this reassurance that if what happened to my mother was to ever happen to me, I would have the power to fight back. I wouldn't become another statistic of domestic violence or femicide, which is what my shrink called it."

"I don't know what that is," he said, laughing to himself, not believing a word coming from my mouth.

"Neither did I," I responded, looking ahead, grasping the weight of the gun in my hand. "It's when a woman is killed by her spouse or ex. Sometimes, just because she's a woman."

"So you're saying someone killed your mom just because she was a woman? Like Jack the Ripper? Ted Bundy?"

"No. That's not—you're misunderstanding."

"So explain it to me."

"There's no time. I have to prevent Elroy Leonard from meeting up with my mother. I'm not supposed to interact with the past. With you or anyone else. I was supposed to be here observing the past through my memories. But somehow, a hypnotist managed to transfer my essence and consciousness back through time and into my teenage self. I can feel and sense and smell everything around me. It's all real. I'm actually back here. I know it sounds like something in one of those science fiction stories you probably read, but it's the truth. I interacted with my mother already and now I have to keep her from being murdered."

"Okay, first off, I don't read science fiction stories. I know I'm a bit weird, but I am not a nerd. Second, if what you're saying is really real, then how can you stop something that already happened?"

"Because it hasn't happened yet. And I'm not going to let it happen," I said. "I'm going to keep it from happening by getting to Leonard first before he gets to my mother. That's why you have to hurry. I'm following a timeline here, and there's not much time left."

"Stop it from happening?" he snapped. "How can you stop it from happening if it happened already like you said? I would like to go back in time and stop myself from answering the door when you rang my bell. But I can't do that because I'm here now driving you to commit murder, which I would be an accessory to."

"I don't have to murder him. I just have to prevent him from meeting up with my mother."

"And what if that doesn't work? Then you shoot him. And I end up going to jail with you because I drove you to and from the scene of the crime. That makes me an accomplice. I know how this works, Anne. I've been watching this new show that premiered last month called Murder She Wrote."

"Nothing's going to happen to you, Steve."

"How do you know? Huh? How do you know? If you're really from the future and in your past self, then you can change things that happened already—just by being here. I was probably home reading a vintage sleaze magazine in the other timeline when this happened. Now I'm here driving a time-traveling vigilante to blow someone away."

"What time do you have?"

He looked at his wristwatch. "Ten after six in my time. I don't know what time it is in time travel time."

He was being sarcastic.

"Just keep going straight," I said to him. "Now, if my memory is accurate, Elroy Leonard should meet up with my mother around six forty-five, while she is on her way to my aunt's house."

Steve looked at his watch again. "You don't have much time," he said.

"I know," I replied. "According to Elroy Leonard's account to the police, he tells my mother to meet him at the abandoned playground. She leaves my aunt's house around eight. Then she drives to meet him at the abandoned playground. She arrives there around eight nineteen. Her time of death was determined to have happened around eight twenty-five that evening. So if we reach the house before that bastard leaves to confront my mother on her way to her sister's house, I can prevent him from ever having that initial contact with her. I have to keep him busy or do something to disrupt the timeline of their initial meeting."

"Something like what?" Steve asked.

"I don't know. Shoot him in the kneecap or shoot out the tires to his pickup. I don't know. Something."

"That still involves jail-time in my future, Anne."

"Just drive."

It took us another fifteen minutes to reach the wooded area where Elroy Leonard lived. It was a rundown neighborhood of single family homes, where low-income families lived.

Elroy's house was beyond a patch of woods, a yard or more from where Steve stopped the car.

"Turn off the engine and wait here for me," I said to him.

"Are you sure this guy lives here?" he asked me.

"My mother gave me and my brother his address and phone number so we would know where she was and how to reach her. I drove out here once before with her. When she was dropping off clothes he left at our house."

I opened the door, and climbed out of the car, stuffing the gun back under my blouse.

"Kill the lights and the engine when I cross the road," I said to Steve.

"Did you have to say kill?"

I dashed across the road and headed toward the trees. Steve watched me go. As I made my way into the woods, I heard his car pulling off. I turned back and watched as he made a complete turnaround and accelerated back up the road we came. I let out a sigh and shook my head in disbelief. *What a coward*, I thought.

I turned back around and headed into the woods, worried more about how much time I had than about getting back home.

I began to see Elroy Leonard's house in the clearing, beyond a thick growth of foliage. I made my way toward it, observing my surroundings. When I reached the door, I stood there a moment, a sudden feeling of anxiety passing through my body. I began to breathe heavy, my hands shaking. *Was I really going to do this?* I asked myself. I took a deep breath, knocked on the door.

I heard the sound of a TV playing inside, then a light came on, and I heard footsteps moving toward the door. A porch light came on, and I heard the chain being removed from the latch on the other side of the door. As the door began to creep open, I placed both of my hands under my blouse and on the gun.

I took a step back as the door opened and my mother's murderer appeared inside, wearing jeans and a plaid shirt. He stood in the doorway with a confused look on his face, almost as if he didn't recognize me.

"Can I help you?" he asked.

Speechless from the terror I felt, I stared back at him, into his dark eyes. I took another deep breath and drew the gun from under my blouse, taking aim. I saw the confused look in his eyes as I pulled the trigger, hitting him center mass in the chest.

He flew backward into the house, dropping to the floor, grabbing his chest. The sound he made as the bullet pierced his body was the worse squeal I had ever heard a human being make. But it was brief. I watched as he gasped for air before his body went limp.

I walked into the house, and stood over him, taking aim again and discharging another bullet into his body. The reverberation of the gunshot rang out with a thunderous clap, causing a painful ringing in my ears. But I ignored it, heaving a sigh of relief as I watched him die.

At that moment, I felt redemption, lifting my head in a gesture to the heavens. I started to walk away when I heard the sudden scream of a woman.

I looked toward the kitchen, taken aback. A woman in a bathrobe stood in the doorway, holding her hands to her mouth.

"Oh, God! Oh, God!" she screamed.

My mouth dropped open and my heart raced in rapid beats the moment I saw her. She was about to run, turning her back to me. My first reaction was to flee, but, in a panic, I raised the gun and fired a shot in her direction, striking her in the back. She fell face first to the floor.

I ran from the house, deluged by a fear I never felt before—a fear that moved my legs faster than I ever remembered moving them. *Congratulations, Anne*, I told myself, *you're officially a murderer.*

CHAPTER ELEVEN

I RAN FROM THE HOUSE and into the woods, looking back to make sure no one was after me. My heart raced. My breaths came in long huffs. I had no sense of direction. I knew I had to get as far away from the crime scene as my legs would take me. Even with the weight of the gun in my hand, I ran faster than a track star in a mile sprint.

Before I knew it, I found myself running along a dark road that lead to nowhere. I found myself rushing along a wooded dirt trail that took me to a lake. It was there that I stopped to catch my breath. I fell to my knees and dipped my hands in the lake to splash water in my face.

I looked around, checking to make sure I was alone.

The night air was stagnant, eerie. Too cold for crickets. Too murky to be seen. I placed my hands over my face and started crying.

"What have I done?" I whimpered.

I removed my hands from my face and the tears poured from my eyes. I looked to the half-moon in the night sky as if its light soothed my anguish. I tried my best to stand, but my legs had become numb from the fear and the grief paralyzed me.

I murdered Elroy Leonard and a woman who was probably his lover. My bitterness and rage had driven me to the point of no return. I acted on an impulse and vindictiveness I had buried in me for thirty years.

The images of the unknown woman kept flashing through my mind, haunting me like a bad dream, and making me feel sick to my stomach. I tried to vomit over the water, but instead, I fell flat on my face into the mire. I didn't move for several long moments. I thought about Andy and my mother. She was safe now, and I had to get myself together to go to her, to see her again. Alive.

I mustered every ounce of strength to get to my feet and start the long walk home. I looked out at the indigo waters, wiping my eyes. The streams were calm, glistening in the moonlight. I tossed the murder weapon into the lake and ran back into the woods.

It took me over an hour to make it back to my old neighborhood. I found myself walking with a limp, staggering along a sidewalk down the street from my house. I didn't notice the police cars parked in front of my home until I looked in that direction.

I slowed my pace, fearing they were there for me. Maybe Steve went to the police. Or maybe they found the bodies at Elroy Leonard's house. Maybe his neighbors heard the gunshots.

I wasn't sure what to do next. Flee or face the music. I didn't know how many hours I had left before Professor Singh brought me out of my trance and back into the present time. If he didn't, I would be arrested and go to jail in this timeline for murdering Leonard and that woman.

I wiped tears from my eyes and walked into the front yard of the house. But I noticed something out of the corner of my eye. I turned and looked toward the driveway and didn't see my mother's car. I saw my aunt's car parked there instead.

A bad feeling rushed through me as I made my way to the front door. I walked into the house and headed toward the living room where two police officers were standing next to my aunt. I recognized both officers. They were the same two policemen who responded to our house when my aunt called the cops after my mother didn't show up at her house.

That was from the original timeline.

But I wondered why they were here *now*? I saved my mother from her killer. Why would the same officers who responded that horrible night be in our house *now*? What made me worry was that everyone was wearing the exact same expressions and standing in the exact same positions and doing the exact same thing they were doing in the original timeline.

But I changed that timeline.

I *killed* Elroy Leonard.

My mother should be home right now.

I looked at my aunt. She was crying and clutching at my uncle's arm. I looked at the two police officers. Their expressions told me they were here delivering bad news.

When my uncle saw me, he rose from the couch and walked over to embrace me.

"Anne," he said.

I looked away from my uncle and toward the dining room area where I saw Andy sitting at the table, slumped in a chair, his head down.

He was still wearing his costume. He wouldn't stop gazing at his jack-o'-lantern. He had that same sullen look the night my mother was murdered. He was sitting in that same chair, wearing his ghost costume and not talking.

I walked away from my uncle and into the living room. "What's wrong?" I asked.

My aunt looked at me, but she didn't answer me. There were tears in her eyes. She rushed through the two officers and out the living room.

"Anne, your mother's missing," my uncle said, his voice cracking. "She was supposed to meet with your aunt at our house over two hours ago, but she never showed up."

"What? That's not possible. She has to be out there. I—she…" I looked toward the Anco wall clock over the fireplace. It was twenty minutes after nine. My mother should have been home by now.

"Maybe she stopped at Eddie and Myrna's house for the party? Maybe she decided to go there."

"No," my uncle said. "We called them. No one at the party has seen her. Everyone there is out looking for her. This isn't like her to disappear without a word."

"Maybe she got a flat somewhere," I said, trying to bring hope into the room. "We should be out looking for her, too."

"We have several patrol units out looking for her," one of the officers said. "We're canvassing every street and neighborhood and parking lot and road all over town."

"She couldn't have just disappeared," I muttered under my breath. I had a revelation: *the parking lot!* When the police officer mentioned parking lots, it hit me. I saw the abandoned parking lot in my mind and panicked. "Oh, no. No. It can't be."

"What, Anne?" my uncle asked. "What is it?"

"No. It just can't be," I repeated. "That can't be it."

I stumbled backward, my hands shaking. I looked around at everyone with wide eyes. I searched the room and saw the keys to my aunt's car on the coffee table. I ran and snatched them from the table, bolting for the front door.

My uncle ran after me. "Anne! Anne, what's wrong?"

I raced out to the driveway and jumped into my aunt's car, starting the engine and putting it in reverse.

"Anne!" my uncle shouted, "Where are you going with your aunt's car?"

I hit the gas and tore out the driveway, putting the car in drive and peeling off.

I knew where I was going. Back to the crime scene. I had to make sure Elroy Leonard, the man who murdered my mother, was dead. I watched him die, but maybe he was pretending. Maybe he wasn't as injured as he led me to believe. Or he was damn lucky. I had to know for sure. My mother wasn't one to vanish and not call anyone. She would always let someone know where she was—family or friend.

During the entire drive, my heart raced from anticipation and fear. I dreaded going back to the scene of the murder, but I had to find out what happened to my mother—if something went wrong and if she deviated from the events of the original timeline. Maybe I messed things up by interacting with her. I had to know for sure.

When I reached the road where Steve had left me, I parked the car near the shoulder and got out. I ran through the woods in the direction of Elroy Leonard's house. I began seeing flashing sirens in the distance through the glade. I stooped low as I neared a patch of foliage, stopping to hide behind a tree as I checked to make sure no one saw me.

Ambulances, police cars and a coroner van surrounded the front of the house. Neighbors had gathered around outside, some wearing robes and nightgowns, while others, dressed in warm clothing and heavy jackets, gathered around the front of the house to see what was going on.

Weary looking detectives in plain clothes were interviewing a few of the spectators, taking notes.

I heard a man yelling and cursing from inside the house. I saw the police bring him out, restraining him, trying to calm him.

"Someone killed them!" he was shouting. "Murdered them! They killed Emmett! They murdered him!" His voice sounded familiar, but I couldn't see his face.

Two police officers led him toward one of the police cars. As they placed him into the back seat, holding down his head to keep him from hitting it against the weatherstripping around the door, the lights from the siren illumined his face. Even though I caught a quick glimpse of him, I recognized his face from my dreams and the courthouse.

It was him. Elroy Leonard.

He was still *alive*.

CHAPTER TWELVE

THE MOMENT I SAW ELROY LEONARD alive, my legs wavered. My hands began to tremble out of control and I stumbled backward, falling to the ground.

I wanted to run, but I was too dazed and stupefied to even make sense of my surroundings. I got to my feet and moved back into the woods, watching the house. I had to make certain no one saw or heard me.

A coroner pulled a gurney with a body bag on it from the house. It had to be the woman I shot. But as they wheeled the corpse toward a parked transportation van, two more coroners appeared, bringing another body bag from the house.

Two bodies?

What the hell was going on?

My eyes went back and forth from Elroy Leonard in the police car, to the two body bags being loaded into separate vans until the reality made sense.

If he was still alive, my mother had to be—

I retreated back the way I had come, trying my best to pick up speed despite the shoes I was wearing. I tripped over my own feet and a few twigs along the way.

One of the police officers at the scene must've heard me, because he shined his flashlight in my direction. But I didn't stop. I kept running, desperate to get back to my aunt's car.

When I reached the car, I got in, started the engine, turned on the headlights and drove back down the road I had come, flooring the gas pedal.

I wasn't sure how to get to where I was going. I had never been there. I knew where the police had found my mother's body, but I had never been there in person, only in my dreams. And in the past, there was no such thing as Mapquest or GPS. I had to depend on landmarks.

The dark roads I took made it difficult to figure out where I was driving. After a half hour, I saw the dilapidated structure of the abandoned factory appearing over some withering treetops.

I accelerated toward it.

I knew the structure. That was where the police found my mother's body. It was adjacent to the parking lot and abandoned playground.

A strange fog encompassed the earth around it—the same fog from my dreams. My heart throbbed in my chest with rapid pangs as I drove through the thickening haze. It engulfed my car and blinded my sight. I turned on the high beams, but they did little to light my way. I began to see headlights from another vehicle as I drove into the abandoned parking lot. My chest tightened as I realized whose car they were coming from.

I took my foot off the gas pedal and allowed the car to roll in the direction of the headlights. As the vehicle crept toward it, I found myself trembling.

I stopped the car, pressing the brake hard. I put the gears in park and got out. The eerie fog made it challenging to see anything around me outside of the high beams of the parked car. I heard the engine idling as I moved at a slow pace toward the headlights. With each step, I felt the fractures in the concrete under my feet. There was death in the air, and it made me cringe.

I realized the distance between me and the running car was further than I thought. The fog began to dispel, allowing me to see the distance I was from the vehicle. At least a yard.

I watched as the heavy haze scattered, granting me passage. It was as if some unseen supernatural force parted the fog for me, wanting me to not only have a clear view of the car, but who was in it.

I recognized the color first. A distinguishable blue. The same color as my mother's car. The dome light was still on, and I could see a person slumped over the steering wheel.

I felt faint, my legs wobbling.

I knew who it was.

I didn't have to take another step forward.

But, how? I asked myself. *How did Elroy Leonard survive two fatal gunshots? How did he get to my mother before I could save her?*

I collapsed to my knees and began crying.

"Why? Why? This—this can't be. How did this happen—*again*?"

For several moments, I was unable to move. I didn't want to move. Until… a voice echoed around me.

"Anne, what have you done?"

I lifted my head and looked around, but no one was there.

I heard it again, clear in my mind.

"I told you this would happen if you, in any way, interrelated with the events of your past. You changed something."

The voice became familiar, and I realized it was Professor Singh speaking to my mind.

I lost awareness and felt my young body go lifeless.

I found myself slipping in and out of consciousness as my thoughts and subconscious mind did a bungee jump from the past to the present. My mind had become a yo-yo through time, from seeing the world through the eyes of my teenage self, to opening my eyes back in Professor's Singh's lab.

He was standing over me, his eyes closed, trying to stay linked to my thoughts.

One of his nurses ran over to him. I saw her as I struggled to regain full consciousness.

"Professor, her vitals are way off. Her heartbeat has elevated. She is not only seeing the memories of her past. She's reliving them! You must bring her back now or we'll lose her."

I heard Professor Singh direct his response to my mind.

"Anne, you've done something to distort the timeline," he said. "I warned you there would be no safe way to repair something broken in the past. You changed the timeline somehow. If I can't get you out of this trance or bring your consciousness and essence back into the present body, you'll end up trapped there and your present self will become an empty shell without a mind or a soul. You'll die here, Anne."

I heard him, but I did not respond in my present body. I saw my mind traveling away from the present, away from that body.

"Anne, if you hear me in your thoughts, you must allow your consciousness to return to your body in the present? Anne...?" His voice began to drift off. "You... must... listen... to... me. You... will... die... here..."

I opened my eyes, sprawled out flat across the ground, looking straight up at the dark clouds blowing in from the East. I no longer heard Professor's Singh's voice. The sound of a car's tires rolling across the pavement was all I heard as I sat up and looked behind me.

The Police had arrived.

CHAPTER THIRTEEN

THEY FOUND MY MOTHER'S BODY way too soon—two days too soon—and that was my fault because I led them right to the scene of the crime. Things were bad enough—with two dead bodies—but somehow Elroy Leonard was still *alive*. And now I was about to be transported to the police station for questioning.

The young cop who sat behind the wheel of the patrol car didn't utter a word. He didn't ask me any questions and he hadn't cuffed me. I wasn't under arrest. Not yet. But I would now have to explain why I was present at two homicide scenes. That wasn't the worse part.

I had changed the events of time and now I was stuck in the past—in my teenage body. If Professor Singh wasn't able to find a way to snap me out of my trance and bring me back to the present, more damage to the timeline would be done. And worse than that, lives that weren't lost in the initial timeline would be lost in this one.

I wondered about the woman. Who she was and why she was at Elroy Leonard's house? *Was she there in the original timeline?* I knew one thing was certain. She didn't die by my hands in the original timeline, but she did in this one. Her blood was on my hands now.

I shuddered at the thought in the back seat. I had to wrestle with my emotions over her death and my mother's.

A horror rose over me—a fright of prison and a concern for Andy. What was he going to do when he discovered mom was dead? When she was murdered before, he shut down and withdrew from life. Would it be the same again? Would I have to watch him go through that hell all over again? How was I going to keep him from becoming a person no longer able to mentally function?

I would lose Andy all over again the same way I lost my mother for a second time. I did more damage than good by traveling back in time. Or I didn't do anything because nothing's changed. My mother was still murdered and her murderer was still alive.

I felt my eyes swelling with the salty wetness of tears again. The more I pondered upon the fate of what was and what was still to come, the greater the grief.

I looked up at the reflection of the police officer's eyes in the rearview-mirror. He was looking back at me, and I saw the empathy eched into his expression.

"Sorry for your loss," he said. "The detectives will get to the bottom of this once I get you to the station. They'll ask some routine questions, then you can go home and be with your family."

Though the tone of his voice and his sincerity were encouraging, I had no response. I looked away from him and stared through the smoked glass window, out into a pitch blackness that moved with the car.

The drive to the police station wasn't long. When we arrived, the young police officer got out, opened the door for me, and escorted me inside.

I had never seen the inside of a police station except in movies. I had imagined them as these dull bunkers with desks, holding cells, water coolers and on-duty officers scattered in an open space. But the interior of this station was designed to be inviting. The two-story structure had high ceilings, bright lighting, wall art and photographs, and an upbeat paint job.

I took a seat in the main lobby while the police officer walked over to the main desk, where he spoke to the desk sergeant, a sour-faced man with a receding hairline and thick glasses. They whispered every word to each other, both glancing back at me during their conversation. That made me uneasy, but I tried not to show it. I kept the tears coming, mourning the loss of my mother. I needed them to feel sorry for me, even though the heartache of losing my mother again gnawed at my soul.

I felt more anxiety and confusion than mourning. I wanted to find out why Elroy Leonard was still alive and who was the woman I shot dead.

After a few moments passed, the young police officer left the lobby, heading back outside to his police car. At the same time, a detective entered the lobby from a room behind the main desk. He wore a white shirt with a black tie and dark gray slacks. His gold shield was attached to his belt, next to his holstered gun. He had graying hair in a slicked-back Mullet style. A popular look from the eighties. He must have been in his mid to late forties. A married man. He wore his wedding band on the correct finger.

He smiled as he approached me, the strong aroma of Old Spice fanning from his pores as he extended his hand to me.

"Miss Donovan? I'm Detective Kelly. I want to offer you my sincerest condolences."

At first I didn't answer him. He used my maiden name. I forgot about that name. I hadn't used that name in years since marrying Tom. I had to pretend to be Anne Donovan all over again. I looked at him and gave a nod, accepting his condolence.

"Thank you," I replied, my voice cracking.

I reached out to shake his hand, and he looked at me with a thoughtful expression.

"I know this is a bad time, but I need to ask you some questions. I hope that's all right?"

I nodded my approval.

"I appreciate that," he said. "Let's go to the back."

I got up and followed him through the main desk area and to a back room, where several other detectives were busy at their desks, making phone calls, writing reports, filing paperwork.

Detective Kelly led me to his desk, which was cramped in a corner toward the back. He kept it simple: typewriter, a lamp, a single photograph of his wife and kids, and an ashtray. Everything was archaic compared to the state-of-the-art computers and police equipment in my time. Maybe that would give me the edge during questioning.

He pulled out the chair for me next to his desk, and I positioned myself in it, crossing my legs, forgetting that I was a teenage girl and not that snooty older woman who married into money in the future.

Detective Kelly took out a pen and sat down behind his desk, removing a writing pad from the desk drawer. Then he got straight down to business.

"I know this is a tough time for you, Miss Donovan—or Anne. Can I call you Anne?"

"Certainly."

"Thanks. Anne, I know you're going through a lot right now, but I need to get some answers concerning your mother. Do you have any idea what happened?"

"She was murdered," I said simply.

"Yes. I'm sorry about that. Did you witness the crime?"

"Not visually," I responded.

"What do you mean?"

"I wasn't there to see it happen, but I saw it happen in dreams. I know every detail."

He cleared his throat. "What details?"

"I saw who did it."

"You saw the murderer? But you said you weren't there."

"I said not visually. In dreams. Bottom line, I know who did it and you have to arrest him before he gets away with it."

"Who are we referring to here?"

"Her ex boyfriend. Elroy Leonard."

He knew who I was talking about. "Leonard?"

"Yes. Leonard."

"Why were you there at the parking lot where the body was found?"

"I was trying to save my mother from Elroy Leonard."

"How do you know it was Leonard when you weren't there to see the crime take place?"

"No one else had a motive."

"You believe that Leonard had a motive to murder your mother?"

"Yes."

"And what do you believe his motive was?" he asked.

"Rejection," I replied simply.

"I'm afraid I can't go off of that. We need more than just an account of a dream you said you had."

"You need to question him," I insisted.

"We will when we build our case."

How long will that take? He's a free man right now. He can get away."

"I doubt if he plans on going anywhere anytime soon. He lost his brother tonight in a double homicide."

"His—his brother?"

"Leonard had a twin brother staying with him from out of town. Someone shot him and his fiancée at Leonard's house."

"Elroy Leonard had a **twin**?"

"Yep. We believe someone murdered his twin—and the fiancée—trying to get to him."

Someone was. Me. I wanted to tell him that—come clean. Let him know I murdered two innocent people to keep Elroy Leonard from murdering my mother. But I didn't want to go to jail. Not yet. Not until Elroy Leonard was caught and brought to justice for what he did.

He had to die. The way he did in the original timeline. But this time, I didn't want my brother pulling the trigger. I had to consider my next step. But first I had to get out of this interrogation.

"Were you there tonight?" Detective Kelly asked.

"Where?"

"Elroy Leonard' house."

"I was there looking for my mother. She wasn't there, so I left. Am I a suspect?"

"I didn't say that."

"Why am I being questioned, then? I just found my mother murdered. I should be home. With my brother."

"We'll get you home to your family. We just needed to ask you some questions first. It's preliminary. You were at two crime scenes tonight."

"I don't see that as a coincidence, detective. I see that as a misfortune. My misfortune."

"Unfortunately, it was, and I'm sorry about that."

"Can I please go home and be with my family. My baby brother needs me right now."

"Sure thing, Anne. I'll get one of the officers to drop you off."

"I can drive myself. Is my aunt's car here?"

"Yes, it is. It's parked outside."

I stood up and started walking toward the entrance door.

"Oh, Anne?"

I stopped and turned to face him.

"What did you mean by you were at the parking lot trying to save your mother? Save her how?"

"By warning her that her life was in danger."

"From Elroy Leonard, I'm assuming?"

"That's right."

"And you know for sure he had intent to harm her?"

"As sure as I'm standing here right now talking to you, detective."

He nodded. "Well, we'll be in touch if there are any developments in the case."

"Thank you, detective."

I turned and left the room.

I had to be careful from here on. The police were going to be watching me.

CHAPTER FOURTEEN

"SHE'S RESISTING ME. She refuses to free her consciousness from the past."

Professor Singh.

I heard his voice echoing in my thoughts again, as if he was in the same room with me.

"Anne, I am trying to bring you back, but you're fighting me. You must let go of the past. I can't bring your consciousness back unless you allow me to. You have to let go of the past."

I felt his fingers compressed against my temples with determined force. I smelled his foreign cologne. But I was unable to see him and unable to respond to him.

"In less than two hours, I will lose you, Anne."

I felt my body adrift in limbo, somewhere between the past and the present. I felt my consciousness drifting across an astral plane between space and time, where substance had no relevance. I floated in a dividing line of reality, whisked away similar to confetti in a strong breeze. I felt my body being swept into a dark vacuum where the laws of Physics had no boundaries.

The resonance of Professor Singh's waning voice filled the void.

"Anne, if I lose you, find me. Find me… find me… it's the only chance you have to undo the damage… find me."

I opened my eyes as blinding fog lights from a car came straight at me. I must've blacked out again from the transference of my consciousness between space and time.

I had little time to react as my aunt's car strayed across the lane into onrushing traffic. It was the blaring horn from the front car that joggled my senses back to life, and back into my nineteen-year-old self. If I hadn't heard it in time, I would have crashed. But I crossed my hands over each other and made a sharp turn in the opposite direction, avoiding a head-on collision as I veered across the road.

I pulled over onto the side of the road and turned off the engine. My body leaned forward as I gripped the steering wheel to stop my hands from trembling. I took a moment to catch my breath and pull myself together. I leaned back in the seat, throwing back my head and taking my hand to sweep strands of my ruffled hair away from my eyes.

I wondered, at that moment, if I had crashed, and my teen body had succumbed to injuries, what would have become of my soul? Where would my consciousness have gone? Would I become a ghost trapped between the past and present?

Either way I looked at it, if I die here, I die in the future. I ruined my chances of returning to my future self, and now I had to come up with a backup plan—one that would guarantee I had a future… and Andy did, too.

I took a deep breath and started the car. I floored the gas pedal and drove toward town.

It took me eighteen minutes to reach the town. The good thing about the past was its lack of technology. No cops out with modern laser speed guns and no traffic cameras mounted to poles or street lights. I got away with driving over the speed limit.

But I had to avoid any run-ins with the police. If they did pull me over, I didn't have my driver's license on me. I left it home along with the rest of my identification cards. I was batting a thousand and taking huge risks from the moment I tried to stop Elroy Leonard from murdering my mother. Now I had changed past events and my own fate was at stake. I realized that matters would get worse if I didn't repair the damage I had done. And the way to do that was by finding Professor Singh in this time.

I pulled the car up to a corner phone booth and got out. I had almost forgotten what they looked like—a rectangle metal and plastic box with windows all around it. I felt as if I was walking into an archaic memento displayed at a museum. I almost forgot how to open the door as I felt around the metal frame for a lever or handle.

Once inside, I reached for the printed phone directory and began scratching through the pages with my long nails. I didn't see any Singhs living in Iowa. I checked out of state listings in another book and found him. He was in Minneapolis, a little over three hours away by car.

I ripped the page from the phone book and rushed back to the car. I opened the door, about to get in, when I noticed something across the street. The perfect twenty-twenty vision of my younger self noticed it right away. My older eyes would have missed it, but my young eyes were as sharp as an eagle's. It was Elroy Leonard's pickup truck. It was parked in front of a local bar.

I recognized the offensive bumper stickers plastered across the rear tailgate. He was the lone person in town who drove a dark green Jeep Gladiator that looked as if it had served Army recruits in overseas combat.

I had no doubt it belonged to Leonard, and no doubt that I had to do something I refused to do before—face him. In the original timeline, during my younger years, I feared him—even before he murdered my mother. I hated him to the point that I didn't want to be anywhere near him.

But that wasn't how I felt now. My abhor and ire steered my footsteps in heavy trudges straight across the street and into the bar.

The moment I entered, I was greeted by country music and a penetrating stench of stale beer and pungent perspiration. Even the lingering clouds of cigarette smoke spiraling in the air did nothing to filter the odor.

This was a place for the blue collar after-work man and the promiscuous woman looking for a free drink and a one night stand. It was filled with the unkindest, stone-faced patrons I had ever seen. The men played pool or darts, while others sat at the bar intoxicating themselves.

The bar had been designed to emulate an old western impression with old weathered Barnwood flooring and wood paneling on the walls. It felt rustic and dated. The smell of the distressed wood prickled the hairs of my nostrils. I wanted to turn around and run away, but the bartender noticed me standing in the doorway, and he grimaced at my presence. I knew I wasn't welcomed. Not because of my look, but because of my age.

He rested his hands on the counter and said, "Can I help you?"

I walked over to the counter, not realizing he noticed my body movements—that I didn't walk with the bounce of a nineteen-year-old girl, but with the mince of a middle-aged woman confident and refined. I looked at him and spoke in an offhand softness.

"Let me get an Alabama Slammer. If you don't have that, I'll take a gin."

He seemed taken aback by my poise. He folded his arms and cocked a brow.

"I need to see some ID first?"

I smacked my hands against my jean pockets and went through my jacket pockets before remembering that I had left my wallet and handbag at home.

"Shit."

"You have to be twenty-one or older to order drinks from the bar," he said.

"Listen, I know this is going to sound like bull to you, but I'm well over the age limit. I just look young."

"I still need to see ID," he insisted.

I sighed, looking away from him.

I spotted Elroy Leonard seated at a booth toward the rear of the bar. He was alone, guzzling down beers. I started walking toward him in slow, hesitant steps.

The bartender grimaced. "Hey! Hey! Where the hell do you think you're going? You're too young to be in here."

I ignored him and walked straight toward Elroy Leonard's booth.

He didn't notice me approaching. His head was down, his eyes gazing from the several empty beer bottles on the table to the picked over plate of food he hardly touched. I saw the anguish in his drooping posture. He was a big man, well over six feet tall, broad shoulders, but the grief that plagued his soul diminished his godly stature. He was hurt. I saw that. But it wasn't over what he did to my mother. It was over his twin.

I felt no remorse for him. If I had the gun on me now, I would have put a hole through his head where he sat. He deserved it.

He looked up at me, and I stood there, catching his pitiful gaze. He seemed at a loss, not knowing what to say, but my presence didn't surprise him. It scared him. He lowered his head again, avoiding eye contact.

I took another step toward the booth, not saying a word. I didn't have to. I knew he felt my hatred from where he sat.

"Sorry about your mom," he said. He grabbed his last bottle of beer and finished it off in a long gulp, his head hitting the back platform of the seat.

When he finished, his eyes roamed everywhere around the booth except in my direction. He knew he was guilty, but I didn't anticipate a confession. Not from him. He was a coward.

"I wish I had comforting words," he said.

Ha! I wanted to laugh right in his face. *Sure you do*, I thought. I sat in the seat across from him and stared at him, waiting for him to look at me.

He didn't.

Instead, he looked around for the waitress.

"I'm going to order some more brews. You, uh, want anything?"

I didn't respond. I didn't break my gaze. I wanted him to feel uncomfortable. I wanted him to sweat.

He gestured to the waitress as she walked over to the bar.

"Hey, waitress, can I get another round over here!" he shouted from the booth. She looked at him and nodded.

I reached over the table and picked up one of the bottles of beer he had drank. I twirled it around in my hand, looking at the label. That made him curious.

I looked into his sullen eyes. "This is the same beer you were drinking that night," I said to him.

He scrunched his face, confused. "Excuse me?"

"The same beer you used to bring to the house when you would stay the night," I said.

"What of it?"

"The same beer you left behind on the playground while you waited for her."

"For who?"

"You know who."

"I don't know what you're talking about."

"Yes, you do." I put the bottle down and leaned forward. "Why did you do it?"

"Do what?"

"Why did you murder my mother?"

His dark eyebrows met with a scowl. He straightened his posture and looked at me shaking his head.

"I didn't murder anybody. I have no idea what you're talking about."

"I always wanted to know why. It was the question that I kept asking myself over and over again. Why? I could see if my mother had cheated on you or threatened you, and even then that wouldn't have given you the right to take her life. No man is above God's sixth Commandment. But you didn't care about her life or how it would affect my life or my brother's. You only cared about yourself. But why? Why? What drove you to do that to her?"

He sprung to his feet, reaching into his pants pocket and pulling out loose bills. "I'm done with this conversation," he said as he threw the money on the table. "You need to go home and be with your family. I'm sure they need you right now."

"*Need!*" I snapped. "Need? I needed my mother and you took her from me!"

I jumped from the booth and stood in front of him, keeping him from walking away from me.

"Can I get past please?" he said, clenching his fist.

"I want an answer from you!" I demanded. "I want to know why! Why?"

"I have nothing left to say to you, little girl."

He tried walking around me, but I grabbed his arm. I felt the tension stiffen his muscles.

"This doesn't end well for you, Elroy Leonard."

He yanked his arm back. "Is that a threat?" he growled.

"It's a promise."

"Little girl, I'm the wrong person for you to be fucking with."

"I'm not afraid of you anymore, Elroy Leonard. I'm going to make sure you pay for what you did to my mother."

"Go home, little girl," he laughed. "That's the safest place for you. And don't ever get in my way again."

He turned away from me and stormed out of the bar.

I bit down on my lip, not realizing my hands had balled into fists. I noticed that the eyes of the bartender and patrons had locked onto me. Everyone was quiet and curious until I shouted out, "What the hell are you people looking at? Mind your own fucking business!"

The waitress came over to the booth and began clearing the table, placing the plate of food and empty beer bottles on a tray.

I looked at the bottles and realized—

"Oh, my god. The beer. The cans in the parking lot. Oh, shit!"

CHAPTER FIFTEEN

I FLEW FROM THE BAR in a straight sprint to my aunt's car. Elroy Leonard had pulled off. I saw the red taillights of his vehicle halfway up the street by the time I reached the car door and opened it. I started the engine, threw the car in gear, hit the gas, and the tires screeched, as the car tore up the street in the same direction he was headed.

I must've blown three lights without easing my foot from the pedal. I kept checking the mirrors to make certain the police weren't following me. But not a single cop car lingered anywhere in town. The town had no crime back in this time. It was a small population of maybe twenty thousand people. Everyone knew each other. Everyone got along. There was never a need for a large police presence. We had one police station in the entire town and three cops worked the evening tour in patrol cars. The chances of seeing a cop cruising through the streets after sunset was not likely. That made driving through the streets at high speeds more in my favor.

Another advantage I had was that I knew where I was going. Driving beyond town had one broad detriment—no street lights. The roads were covered in darkness, and the moon was obscured by a ceiling of dense, stagnant clouds.

As I drove along the countryside, even the silhouettes had vanished. The night turned the main plank road into a blanket of darkness. I had to measure distance by sight from the expanse of the high beams. If anything was out there in the night, I wouldn't be able to see it in time to brake.

I paid no attention to the night as I drove. I didn't realize how fast I was going until, out of the night's smoky obscurity, headlights from another vehicle came right at me. My eyes widened as I removed my foot from the gas pedal and tried to swerve.

But it was too late.

The oncoming vehicle sideswiped me, causing me to lose control.

The car flipped over to its side and into a ditch, knocking me around as if I was a ragdoll. I felt my forehead smash against the steering column and the bone snap in my right wrist. My legs locked, and my foot abandoned the brake as the car fell upside-down in the ditch. Blood trickled from my nose and the skin of my forehead split into an open wound that oozed an onslaught of blood.

I slumped over onto my side, dazed, in and out of consciousness. For a long moment, my body didn't respond to attempts to move. I felt the blood flowing from my forehead, and the heat from the car, as the engine continued to rev. I didn't smell gas or see smoke, which meant I didn't have to worry about an explosion. But, for a few seconds, I didn't feel my legs. And I had no sense of my surroundings. My lip and tongue were bleeding and the taste of the coppery fluid melded in my mouth.

I tried reaching for the door lever on the passenger's side, but I screamed out in pain. I realized more than my wrist was broken. My entire right arm was numb. I lifted my head and heard a snap in my neck. It wasn't broken, but the more I strained to elevate my head an inch, the more pain I felt searing through my neck, shoulders and back. I had no choice but to use my legs, raising them from the floor and placing my feet against the driver's side door. I pushed my legs forward until I reached the door handle with my left hand.

I gripped my entire palm around it, squeezing each finger tight into a clenched fist until the door opened. I used whatever strength I had in my upper body to drag myself across the seat and out the car. I fell face-first into the ditch. My left arm took the brunt of the tumble, bruising my elbow. Sharp pains shot through my back and shoulders. I had to let out a shriek. The pain was unbearable.

I felt someone grab the back of my jacket and drag me out of the ditch and onto the road.

Whoever it was came and stood over me, their rugged and scuffed hiking boots in my face. I felt the person reach down, grab my jacket again, and turn me over onto my back.

My eyes took some time to focus, but when they did, I saw who it was, and I gasped. It was Elroy Leonard. He hadn't saved me. He had come to kill me. And I was in too much pain to defend myself.

He bent down onto one knee and grabbed me by my blouse, shaking me as if I was a difficult suspect refusing to answer questions in an interrogation. When he finished, he released me, and my body smacked the ground.

He stared down at me, growling, knowing he had me right where he wanted me. He reached into his pocket and pulled out a cigarette, placing it in his mouth. But he didn't light it. He wanted to savor watching me helpless and in pain.

"I could break your fucking neck right now and tell the authorities it happened in the accident," he sneered. "But I tell you what. I'm not gonna do that. I'm a let you live. I'm a let you go home to be with your family. To bury your mother. Outta respect for her memory. That's the only reason why I'm a let you continue to breathe."

In pain, I turned over to my side and spit blood from my mouth.

"What's with you anyhow?" he asked. "Why the hell are you bothering me? Why the hell were you chasing after me?"

I tried to move my leg, but I was in too much agony. I wanted to respond with a kick to his groin, but my body wouldn't let me. Instead, I held my wrist, rolling back and forth moaning.

He looked at me shaking his head. His look told me what he was thinking. He had the upper hand. I was at his mercy.

He got to his feet, taking the cigarette from his mouth and putting it into the upper pocket of his flannel shirt.

"When I finish taking care of business, I'll let the police know you're here so they can send an ambulance," he said. "Consider this a favor of mercy. I'm only doing it out of respect for your mother. Don't follow me again."

He was about to walk away.

I found the strength to lift my upper body and speak.

"It doesn't matter what you do!"

He stopped to look back at me.

"You won't get away. Death is in your destiny, you piece of shit."

I fell back to the ground in pain.

He snickered under his breath and walked back over to me, kicking me hard with his dirty boots. The blow caught me in the chin, almost knocking my teeth out. I remember spitting blood before closing my eyes and losing consciousness.

When I opened my eyes again, I was in a hospital room, on a bed with IV's and monitors on both sides of me. The first thing I saw was the face of my aunt sitting in a chair next to my bed. She smiled the moment I opened my eyes.

"Hey, sweetie, you had us worried," she said.

My uncle appeared behind her, happy to see me awoke.

"You did have us worried," he said.

I looked past him, looking for Andy. I didn't see him.

"Where's Andy?"

"He's fine," my uncle replied. "He's with neighbors. They're watching him for us."

I nodded my approval, while trying to sit up. My right arm was in a cast from my wrist to my elbow. Every bone in my body ached.

"How long have I been here?" I asked.

"Well, the police received a call from a man who told them there was an accident," my aunt answered. "When they got there, they found you unconscious on the road. They called an ambulance and rushed you here. You've been here for a little over three hours."

"I need to go."

I tried to get out of bed, but they stopped me.

"Whoa, young lady, you're not ready to go anywhere, just yet," my uncle insisted, pinning me back down with his arms.

My aunt stood over me brushing back my hair.

"The doctor has to do X-rays to see if you need surgery," she informed me. "You have to stay here overnight. You may be here for another day or two."

"I can't do that," I said. "I have to go now."

"Anne, your wrist is broken, your ankle fractured, and you have a concussion," my aunt said. "You have bruises all over your body. You're in no condition to go anywhere."

"That's right," my uncle agreed. "You need time to heal."

When I realized they would keep me from leaving, I stopped fighting them. I reclined into the bed with a sigh.

"If you're worried about the funeral arrangements, don't," my aunt said, her voice cracking. She looked down at her hands. They were shaking. This wasn't easy for her. She lost her sister. Her eyes watered from the emotional wounds. "Your uncle and I will take care of everything. My sister would want it that way anyway."

"We're not going to move you and Andy out of the house until after the funeral," my uncle added. "You two will stay with us. It's for the best. We'll wait until you heal."

I stared up at the ceiling. I didn't want to talk about this. I lived through it in the other timeline. I wanted to get out of the hospital and make sure Elroy Leonard met his fate. He was too dangerous to remain free.

"I'm sorry about the car," I said to my aunt, changing the subject.

"Don't worry yourself over that," my uncle replied. "We can get that fixed. You just need to focus on getting better. I need for you to do that, okay? That's all that matters."

My aunt, tearing, reached over and rubbed my shoulder.

I looked at her with a smile. "I'll be okay."

My uncle walked over to my aunt and placed his arm around her. That was his way of telling her it was time for them to go. She nodded to him.

"We have to leave now, sweetie," she said. "We'll be back in the morning."

"Of course," I said.

She leaned over to kiss me on the cheek. I smiled. My uncle came over and kissed me on the forehead.

"You get your rest now, okay?" he said, forcing himself to smile. It was his way of hiding his pain.

"I will."

I faked a smile to hide the frustration I felt inside. I didn't want to upset them by letting them see how angry I was. I had to focus on my next move, and not on my physical and emotional pain.

I watched my aunt and uncle head into the hallway where Detective Kelly appeared with a folder in his hand.

"Detective," my aunt said, surprised to see him.

"Good to see you," he said. "I just have to ask your niece some questions concerning the accident. Basic follow up stuff."

"Sure," my aunt said. She looked back at me. "Don't forget, Anne. You need your rest. We'll be back in the morning."

I nodded.

Detective Kelly gave my aunt a nod of assurance. "It won't take long."

She smiled, then left, holding my uncle's hand.

Detective Kelly entered the room and stood at my bedside, opening the folder, but refusing to sit down.

"Sorry to bother you at this time, Anne," he said.

"It's fine, detective," I responded.

"I, uh, just have some questions about the accident."

"Sure. What do you need?"

"Did you see the other vehicle that hit you?"

"Of course I did."

"You did see it?" he seemed surprised. "Did you get a plate? Can you remember the make and model?"

"All you have to do is go to Elroy Leonard's home," I said.

"Elroy Leonard?" he cocked a brow.

"He should have damage to the driver's side of his vehicle where he sideswiped me," I told him. "I'm sure his vehicle scraped paint from my aunt's car."

"Did you actually see Mr. Leonard?" he asked.

"Of course I did," I replied.

"Funny. He didn't report being in an accident."

"Why would he, detective? Especially when he's the one who caused the accident. These bruises on my face are courtesy of his size twelve boot."

"I see." He started writing in the folder.

I waited for him to finish.

"Did Mr. Leonard say anything to you or try to help you at the scene?" he asked.

"He was trying to get back to where he murdered my mother," I said, raising a brow. "So he was kind of in a rush."

"Do you have proof he murdered your mother?" he asked.

"There was proof," I said. "Did your men search the crime scene? Did they find any empty beer cans laying around?"

"It's still an active crime scene, Anne."

"Did you search the playground yet?"

"Not yet."

"Then the beer cans aren't there anymore. He got to them first and probably disposed of them already." I sighed. "And I led him right to them."

"I'm confused here, Anne. You led who to what? What's so important about empty beer cans?"

"On the night Leonard murdered my mother, he was drinking beer while he waited for her in the abandoned playground. Two days after the murder, you found those beer cans and brought them to your lab for processing. You were able to find Leonard's fingerprints all over the beer cans, placing him at the scene of the crime. That led you to interrogate him. He didn't confess, but you found some flaws in his story. You investigated, then got a court warrant to search his house. That's where you found the knife he used to stab my mother in the neck. You were going to bring him in for further questioning, but he tried to run. He was later picked up in another county for speeding, and that's when those police officers saw that he had an arrest warrant. You went and picked him up and brought him back for interrogation. That's when he confessed to the crime."

He stood there agape, a blank look on his face. "I—I don't remember any of this happening," he stammered. "We never interrogated or arrested Elroy Leonard for any crime. I don't—"

"It already happened," I said. "In another time. But I screwed things up. I changed events."

He stood there with his mouth open, staring at me as if I had beamed in from another planet. "Maybe you need to rest. The doctor said you sustained a serious concussion in the accident."

"I'm not crazy, Detective Kelly," I said. "I can't convince you that Elroy Leonard is the man who murdered my mother. But if I'm telling you this, then you need to investigate. You need to interrogate him. You need to ask yourself, who else would have a motive to harm a woman who didn't have an enemy in this world. You can't afford to let him get away. Other lives are at stake. Other women can become victims."

He closed the folder and frowned. "The investigation into your mother's murder is ongoing. Right now, all I can promise you is that we're doing our best." He had a solemn look, but he didn't write me off as crazy. I knew that much about him. I knew he cared.

"You need to get some rest and focus on getting better. I'll check into your story about Leonard. I'll have some uniformed officers check his vehicle for damage. I'll be in touch."

He turned and left the room.

Once he was gone, I took a deep breath, staring up at the ceiling. I knew he cared, but he didn't believe me, and it was up to me to correct the mistakes I had made. But first, I had to get out of the hospital.

I sat up in bed, removing the IV tubes from my arms. In pain, I climbed out of bed and limped toward a closet door, opening it and reaching inside for my clothes.

Every move was slow and aching. I had a cast on my wrist, a bandage around my ankle, and my head was spinning.

I felt every sharp pain in my back and ribs. My younger body had been damaged and bruised, and, as I tried to slip into my jeans, I yelled out in agony. But I didn't let that stop me. I had to undo the damage I had done to the past. That meant finding Elroy Leonard. And I had no choice but to turn to Steve Mitchell for help—again.

CHAPTER SIXTEEN

WHEN STEVE MITCHELL OPENED his front door and saw me standing on his porch banged up, he threw his hands into the air and let out a loud sigh.

"Damnit!" he said, "Okay, okay, first off, answer me this: is the *granny* you still trapped inside the young sexy you?"

I nodded. "I am."

"Oh, man!"

"I need your help, Steve."

"Whatever it is, I don't want to have anything to do with it. Why do you think I drove off and left you? If that wasn't a big enough hint for you, then me going back inside the house and closing the door in your face should clear up any confusion you might have."

"Please, Steve. I need a place to stay for a day or two. That's it. I'll pay you if I have to. But you're the only person who I can turn to. There's no one else."

After a moment, he stepped out onto the patio deck.

"How? I live with my parents. I'm eighteen and a half years old. Where am I supposed to hide you? My parents wouldn't believe I had an elderly teenager hiding in my room. Why can't you stay at your house?"

"Elroy Leonard murdered my mother."

His mouth dropped open and, for a moment, the shock immobilized his body. He stammered under his breath, his eyes searching mine for truth, and when he realized what I told him was real, he placed his hand behind his head and rubbed his neck.

"Oh, man."

He glanced at me.

"How?" he started to say, but he didn't know how to put his emotions into the proper words. Instead, he let out a deep breath and sat on the railing. He tried to process his own disbelief. He looked up at me and said, "I thought—I thought you were here—I thought you were going to prevent that from happening."

"I thought I was, too," I replied with my head down.

"I'm sorry, Anne. Really. Now I feel bad about leaving you out there. I was just scared."

"I understand. I know you were."

"How are you holding up?"

"Not well. As you can see."

"What happened to you?"

"Well, I found out that Elroy Leonard had a twin brother, who I killed because I thought he was Leonard. I also killed an innocent woman in a panic. So, needless to say, I messed up. And to make it worse, I confronted Leonard and I think that he's after me now."

"Does he know what you did?" he asked. "Does he know you whacked his twin and this woman?"

"He doesn't know that. Not yet. But he knows I know he murdered my mother." I walked toward the end of the porch, my left hand gripped around my cast. "He almost killed me last night for confronting him."

"Is that how you got banged up? Did he do that to your hand?"

"It happened in the car accident. He ran me off the road last night. He was trying to keep me from going to the abandoned playground."

"Why were you going there?" Steve asked as he walked up behind me, his hands in his pockets.

"To get to the beer cans he left behind," I answered.

"Beer cans?"

"In the original timeline, he left several empty cans of beer at the abandoned playground where he waited for my mother to arrive. Two days after the police discovered my mother's body, they found those cans and took them in to be examined. They found his fingerprints on them. That's what initially led them to him."

"Oh, wow." He looked down, rubbing his chin in deep thought for a moment. His head snapped to attention as he realized: "What about the beer cans? Where are they?"

"It's safe to say he got to them last night," I answered. "He probably disposed of them. Put them in a place where the police would never find them."

"So what happens now?" he asked.

"I have to go after Leonard before he comes after me."

"That sounds dangerous," Steve said. "Good luck with that. Sorry I can't take that journey with you, but I'm in my first semester right now and I have examines coming up."

I fell silent for a moment, staring across the street at my house.

"You know, I remember what it was like growing up in that house as a girl. I remember rolling around in leaves around this time of the year. I remember playing hopscotch in the street and riding my bike up and down the neighborhood."

Steve looked at me and placed his hand on my shoulder for comfort.

"My life began here in this simple place, during a simple time. This place was home for me. Then Elroy Leonard came along and took that away from me."

I sat on the railing, one leg up, bringing my cast arm to my chest. I closed my eyes and inhaled the morning air. My lungs became filled with its crisp chill. Then I opened my eyes with an exhalation, appreciating the blended hues of the sunrise.

Steve waved his hand to get my attention, and I turned toward him.

"You okay?" he asked.

I cleared the wetness building in my nostrils with a sniffle and wiped a tear from my eye. I stepped down from the railing. "Yeah, fine," I said. "Just considering my options."

"You make everything sound so yesterday," Steve said.

"For me it is," I replied.

"Not right now it isn't," he said, his tone encouraging. "You're here now—again. Right? Reliving it."

"If I had it to do all over again, I would've chosen a more simpler and joyous time. I would have gone back a little farther. Maybe that's what I should have done."

"Yeah, but, you still would've had to relive this nightmare at some point in your life," Steve said. "It almost seems as if it was inevitable."

Steve moved toward me, his motions nervous, yet sympathetic.

"Maybe we can work together and come up with a way to fix things," he suggested.

I looked at him, smiling. I gave him a nod, letting him know that would work for me.

"But first, I have to hide you in the one place I know my parents would never dare look."

I followed Steve into his house and down a flight of steps that led to the basement. We walked toward a door that he had to push with his entire body to enter. The room was dark until he turned on the ceiling light. Dirty clothes were piled in front of the door as if they had been dumped there months ago. And the stench made me feel as if I had entered the locker room of musky males after gym.

"*This*," he said with emphasis, "is the one place my folks would never look for you in the house."

"I see why," I said, not surprised by the mess.

He had the typical teenage male room: discarded candy wrappers and magazines were scattered across his desk and bed. Every magazine cover had either images of hot rods or hot girls. He dove for the hot girl covers first, grabbing them into a pile with his arms and dropping them into a black oversized storage trunk at the foot of his bed.

He looked at me, his face blushed red from embarrassment. He swept his arm across the bed to remove the dirty clothes and hot rod magazines.

"Sorry about the mess," he said. "I never have company."

"I wonder why?" I said, being sarcastic. I walked into the room scoping the model cars he had displayed on wall shelves, each one handcrafted from scratch.

"You made those?" I asked him.

He looked toward the shelves. "Me and my dad," he answered, a sense of pride in his tone. "Dad and I love hot rods."

"Is it a hobby?" I pried.

"Not really," he responded. "Just quality time with my pop, really. He loves working on models. I love working on the real thing."

"Quality time with your parents are important," I said. He knew I was referring to my own mother. I spoke in a hushed tone, and my sadness was obvious.

He finished clearing his bed and offered me a seat, patting the mattress.

"You can sit right here, if you like," he said.

I sat on the bed, continuing to look around the bedroom, scanning the walls covered with posters and photographs and newspaper clippings.

The wood-panelled walls and eighties teen movie posters brought back fond memories of a time I once cherished. I felt young again—and that felt weird, considering I was in my teenage body.

I was hiding out in the bedroom of a boy young enough to be my son—or worse—my grandson. But when he looked at me, he didn't see the middle-aged woman I was. He saw a teenage girl he wanted to make out with and bring his sexual curiosity to an end.

The thought repulsed me. Even more when I noticed his eyes lusting in my direction.

He turned away, pretending to clean his room, but I knew what he was after, and I thought it was cute. I smiled.

"So, tell me, Steve, do you have a girlfriend yet?"

He blushed. "Not really."

"Why not?"

"Seriously? Look at me. I'm the epitome of a dork. All of the girls during high school only went out with the jocks. Girls are just not interested in me unless they're looking for a free ride to their boyfriend's house or the mall."

"Come over here and sit down next to me," I urged him, patting the bed.

He hesitated.

"Come on. I'm just going to talk to you."

He took slow steps toward the bed, but when he sat, it was at the foot of the bed.

"I used to be a teenage girl once."

"You kind of still are."

"Physically, yes, but when I was a teenage girl I remember most girls having crushes on boys who were either cute, tough or athletic. We didn't notice the smart boys because we still had some growing up to do. Some girls can be fickle. We don't appreciate the good boys until we're damaged by the bad ones. When you go off to college and mature, you'll get noticed. Girls will look beyond the physical and see your personality and potential. Watch. It always happens that way."

"Okay, I have to be honest with you. Right now, I kind of feel like I'm being comforted by my mom."

I laughed. "Sorry about that."

"No, it's okay. Really. It's just that I literally had this conversation with my mom after I graduated high school."

"Sorry." I leaned back on the bed. "So, is there anything you want to talk about?"

"Well, I think we need to talk about you."

"Me?"

"Yeah. I mean you're the granny time traveler who messed up your timeline. How are you going to fix it?"

I got up from the bed, moving toward a desktop globe Steve had on a nearby three drawer dresser. I began spinning it with my fingers. "I need to find the man who sent my consciousness and essence back to this time. He's in Minneapolis. Over three hours away. He may have the ability to return me to my future self."

"How old would he be now?"

"Around our age. Still in college, if I'm right."

"That's kind of young," he pointed out. "Do you think he has these abilities at a young age?"

"I don't know," I said. "I'm hoping he does. He should. He told me to find him in this time, so I'm assuming he does."

"What if he doesn't? What then?"

"I'll be stuck here in this body."

"But what happens to your future body? The *grandma* body?"

"I don't know."

"Well, I know one thing for sure," he said.

"What's that?" I asked.

"You can't live out the rest of your life here in my room."

"I wasn't planning to," I laughed.

"Well, what about food? Have you eaten anything?"

"Come to think of it, I haven't eaten, bathed or slept since my consciousness entered my younger body. I haven't been tired or hungry. But I can sure use a shower."

"You can do that before my parents get home. What about the cast?"

"I can shower with it, but I need to remove it."

"Why? Your arm's broken."

"Just my wrist. It's fractured. I'm going to have to deal with the pain. This thing has to go. I need both hands for what I have to do."

"Uh-oh," he sighed, rolling his eyes. "I don't think I like the sound of that. Two hands for what? Or maybe I shouldn't ask."

I turned to face him. "I can't make you understand what it is I have to do. I wasn't supposed to come back in time to change things. I was supposed to heal myself. But I let my emotions dictate my actions. Now I either have to mend the damage I've done or answer for what I've done. What can I tell you? I'm scared. I'm afraid. I let the man who murdered my mother get away with it. And now I have to find a way to stop him."

Steve didn't have a response. He scratched his head, trying, I guess, to figure out what we should do next. I knew he would help me despite his reservations.

"This is really crazy," he said. "This whole hypnotic time travel stuff and you having to change events that you say already happened. Now you're stuck in the past and you need to find some guy to help you get back to your body which is soulless in the future. Wow. Too much. And I'm sitting here believing every word."

"I'm sorry I got you involved," I said.

"No, no, it's actually okay," he said, jumping to his feet. "I needed to get a life. All I do is work on my car and avoid getting a job."

He brought another smile to my face.

"So what do you wanna do next?" he asked.

"I need to go to Elroy Leonard's house," I answered.

"Are you insane? Why?"

"I need that knife he murdered my mother with."

CHAPTER SEVENTEEN

STEVE PARKED IN THE SAME SPOT the night he left me.

He turned off the engine and got out the vehicle. He wasn't planning on leaving me this time. He opened the trunk and pulled out a musty old army duffle bag. He unzipped it and started pulling out Boy Scout survival kits—binoculars, a canteen, Swiss Army knife, and a compass.

"What are you doing?" I asked him. "What's all that for?"

"Two years ago I saw this movie called First Blood with this guy named John Rambo and—"

"—We don't need all of that stuff, Steve," I said to him, cutting him off. "Just bring the binoculars."

I rushed away from the car and headed into the woods. Steve followed. He ran out of breath trying to keep up. My legs were stronger and faster than his.

I followed the trail I had used earlier to Elroy Leonard's house. In a matter of minutes, we cleared the woods. Leonard's house sat in the distance, across the road. There were two police cars parked in front of it.

I ducked behind a growth of hedge plants. Steve went down on one knee behind me. I grabbed the binoculars from him and focused in on Elroy Leonard's house.

"What's going on?" Steve asked. "Why are the police there?"

"I don't know. Stay low."

I gripped my hands around the lenses of the binoculars and pinned them to my eyes, adjusting the focus on Leonard's front door. A moment later, the door opened and Detective Kelly walked out with another detective and two uniformed police officers.

Elroy Leonard appeared in the doorway, walking behind them. He had his hands in the pockets of his jeans, grimacing. But he wasn't in handcuffs.

He shook Detective Kelly's hand and watched them as they got into their vehicles and drove away. I had no idea what was going on. Maybe Detective Kelly followed my suggestion and decided to question Leonard. Maybe he had some evidence for a case against him.

Whatever was going on, Leonard didn't look happy. He frowned as he went back into his home, slamming the door behind him.

I handed the binoculars back to Steve and moved into a prone position across the ground.

"What now?" Steve asked me.

"We wait," I answered him.

"For what?"

"For Elroy Leonard to leave."

"How long is that going to be?" he asked, shivering. "It's cold out here."

I took the binoculars from him again and looked toward the house. "You can huddle close to me if you want to?"

He wanted to. His eyes locked at my body, widening with excitement, but when he remembered I wasn't the Anne he was attracted to—that girl close to his age who he drooled over, he backed off, keeping his distance.

"I'll be okay," he muttered, shaking from the frost in the air.

"Suit yourself," I said to him, continuing to look through the binoculars.

After a few moments, he came and sprawled his body next to mine, blowing into his hands to keep them warm.

"See anything yet?" he asked.

"Not yet," I replied.

We waited for another five minutes, not a word between us, until Elroy Leonard appeared again, plodding from his house to his truck. The ire in his movements were obvious. Something pissed him off. He got into his vehicle and slammed the door shut. He started the pickup and sped off.

I handed Steve the binoculars and got to my feet.

"Wait here," I said to him. "I'll be right back. And don't leave me this time."

"I won't," he promised.

"I'm trusting you, Steve," I said. "I need for you to be my lookout."

"I can do that. Don't worry."

"If Elroy Leonard comes back, get to your car and honk the horn," I said, looking toward Leonard's house. "But don't wait around for me. Just go. Get to the police station and send them back here. Okay?"

"Okay."

I started to rush off when he said, "Be careful."

I stopped and looked back at him. I reassured him with a smile.

"I will. Make sure you stay out of sight."

He nodded, and I turned away, shuffling my way through the woods and toward Elroy Leonard's house.

I crept up to the front door and tried turning the knob. The door was locked. I looked around for another way in.

I tried the front window next, but it was stuck. Years of dirt and grime had sealed it shut. The glass was plastered with timeworn stains that blackened it, making it difficult to see inside the house. I prowled my way toward the side of the house and tried two other windows. Same thing. I decided to walk around to the rear of the house. I noticed the cellar doors were open.

I headed in that direction.

Before making my way down the steps, I looked around the yard—at the scrap cars and dilapidated garage and wilted grass over a mucky terrain. Elroy Leonard didn't take care of his property. Either he didn't give a damn or he was too busy drinking. Maybe, I thought to myself, the neglect signified his gritty nature. Maybe it symbolized who he was as a person. My shrink would have associated the two had she been here to see how he lived. She would have linked his mistreatment of his property to his nasty and violent temperament.

I tried avoiding trash cans and waste strewn across the backyard as I moved toward the cellar doors, making sure no one else was nearby. I didn't want to assume Leonard was the only one home. If he had more relatives, or a friend, they could be in the house. I had to be cautious. I had to watch the neighboring houses, as well. I didn't know who lived in those adjacent houses or if anyone was home, looking out their windows, watching his property.

I moved hunching my back, staying low, tiptoeing my way to the cellar doors. When I reached them and looked down into the pitch blackness, I had second thoughts. I had no idea what waited for me down there. And worse, I had no way of seeing a damn thing in the darkness. I didn't have a flashlight or cigarette lighter. I would be blind.

I took a deep breath and poked out my chest, stepping down into the blackness. I almost lost my footing on the second step down. The concrete was old, fractured.

I started using my free hand to feel my way through the darkness. The cellar had no windows to welcome light from the surface. Despite the cautious steps I made forward, I stumbled over storage boxes and rusted yard tools. The smell of mold and dank moisture aggravated my nostrils. My eyes watered, and my nostrils flared from the pungent odor. I felt a twitching in my cast arm. It was difficult holding it up while walking.

Something inside of me kept warning me to retreat, but thoughts of my mother flashed across my mind. I failed her and I allowed the man who murdered her to get away with it. I changed the past. Now I had to make amends and bring Elroy Leonard to justice. That motivated me to continue taking bold steps forward.

I walked into a cobweb the size of a fishing net and found myself letting out a shriek. I used my cast to wrench it from the ceiling and away from my face.

I moved on, nervous, hesitant, looking back toward the sooty stream of daylight spilling down into the cellar from the opened doors.

When I turned away from it, my hand felt a cord dangling from the ceiling. I wrapped it around my balling fist and yanked on it. A dull, yellowish light shimmered from the bare bulb and exposed the crypt I was in.

It was more than a basement—more than a crawl space used for storage. Elroy Leonard had turned it into a prohibition venture. He had Lab equipment—glass tubes, beakers, Bunsen burners, large plastic containers, funnels—and several household products situated on wooden worktables and lined in rows across racks and rotted wall shelves.

I didn't know a lot about drugs or alcohol, but I knew enough to know that Elroy Leonard was using his cellar to home brew alcohol and produce illegal methamphetamine.

He was more than a murderer. He was a drug dealer.

I doubt if my mother knew. She would've mentioned it to me or my aunt after she ended her relationship with Leonard. She never did. I doubt if she ever had a chance to witness his dark side outside of the drinking and jealousy. Some men knew how to hide their demons. Leonard was one of those men.

It made me wonder what other shady circumstances would I discover about Leonard the longer I remained in the past? I knew one thing for certain—he wouldn't hesitate to take a life. And that's why I had to be cautious.

I was on his home turf, where he had the advantage. I needed to shift my focus back to the reason why I was at his house. I didn't know how much time I had before he would return.

I began walking through his home brewery, the dust in the air reddening my eyes and triggering my allergies. I had to squint as I explored the cellar for a way to the ground floor, and hold my nose to keep from sneezing.

When I made my way past several storage boxes and piles of junk, I spotted old, rotted wooden stairs leading up to the main floor of the house.

I tested the first step for resilience the moment I reached it. It creaked, but tolerated my weight. The good thing was that I weighed a hundred and eighteen pounds in my teenage body. And I was light on my feet. I moved up the rest of the stairs with the same caution and slink motion as I did the first step until I reached the door. With my good hand, I opened it. But no matter how careful I was, the squeak of the rusted hinges resonated with more squeal.

If someone had been home, I would have been discovered.

I looked at the cast on my arm, knowing I was in no condition to defend myself with a fractured wrist and no gun. But not having a gun made me feel more relieved than uneasy. I didn't want a repeat of the night I killed Leonard's twin and the woman he was with.

The carpet in the living room still had blood stains soaked into it, and the wall still had the splattered blood stain from the woman. I felt the guilt and pain all over again. I knew I had to straighten my posture and move on. I didn't know how much time I had.

I headed toward the kitchen, noticing the pile of dirty dishes Leonard left in the sink. The floors were grubby and the tile cracked.

He kept a shabby house, neglected through time. Symbolic of his personality. Dirty, slimy and inadequate.

I rushed in the direction of the kitchen counter and went through the draws—all of them. It was going to take some time. I had to use my one good hand to move through each drawer.

Ten minutes must have gone by when I heard the faint sound of a car horn blowing from outside. At first, I didn't pay attention to it. I moved through drawers and cabinets as fast as possible, determined to find the weapon Elroy Leonard used to kill my mother. I went through every part of the kitchen when the horn signaled again that someone was coming.

I stopped what I was doing and made my way back into the living room and to the front window. Despite the dirt and grime I saw Leonard's pickup truck pulling up outside.

Shit! I thought. *Too soon.*

I rushed to the door leading back into the cellar. I was about to make my escape back the way I had entered the house, but I froze. I wasn't about to leave empty handed. I closed the door, looked around for a place to hide.

I turned and noticed the door to Elroy Leonard's bedroom was cracked open. I raced in that direction. The stench of mildew and old socks pinched my nostrils. But I didn't grimace. I had to find the perfect hiding place.

I checked under the bed first. He had too many boots and tools under it. I rushed to his closet door. It was crammed with clothes.

I knew I had to find another room. I hurried back toward the hallway, but I heard Leonard's keys jingling in the front door. I jumped behind the bedroom door, breathing heavily, scanning the room for another escape route.

The window.

It was cracked open. If I got to it, opened it, I would have an escape route.

But I ran out of time.

The front door opened and Elroy Leonard walked into the house.

I held my breath and slid down the wall, moving my head to peek through the gap between the door and the frame.

I saw Leonard, putting his keys back into the pocket of his denim jacket.

He was heading for the hallway, coming straight for me—pulling a knife from his back pocket.

CHAPTER EIGHTEEN

I RECOGNIZED THE KNIFE Leonard twirled through his fingers. It was the same knife from my dreams—the one he used to murder my mother. When I saw it, I shoved my body away from the gap and pasted myself against the wall, holding my breath.

As Leonard reached the door, the phone rang. He stopped and grunted, "Who the hell?"

He turned and headed into the kitchen to answer it.

Since he had no idea I was in his house hiding, that worked to my advantage. I let out my breath and sighed in relief. But now I had to consider my next move without getting caught.

I heard faint chatter from his phone conversation through the wall. His heavy boots began pacing the floor. He was still angry about something, and I wanted to know what it was. I placed my ear to the wall, trying to make sense of what was being said between him and the person on the phone.

Leonard, however, was grumbling his words, his voice a hiss of disagreements.

I got to my feet and, in short steps, moved from behind the door and out into the hallway. I kept my back against the wall as I moved little by little toward the opening to the kitchen.

I caught a glimpse of Leonard's shadow move across the floor. He was pacing his way into the hallway.

I hastened to get back into the bedroom, where I ducked behind the door again.

I peeked through the gap and saw Leonard, holding the phone to his ear with one hand and still twirling the knife with the other. He returned the knife to his back pocket and yanked on the telephone cord, extending it to reach the living room.

I heard his conversation with improved clarity from there.

"Yeah," he said into the phone. "They showed up at my door this morning, asking me questions about my relationship with her. They started asking me about my whereabouts the night she was murdered. They asked me if I had any alibis. Can you believe this crap? All because that little bitch daughter of hers told them I had something to do with her mother's murder."

At that moment, I smirked, feeling euphoric. Detective Kelly followed my suggestion. But he had no evidence to bring Leonard in. I had to get him that evidence. But there was a new problem I faced: that evidence was in Leonard's back pocket.

"I need to take care of some stuff first," Leonard said into the phone as he paced the floor. "Bury my brother and his old lady. Then take the bodies back to Missouri. No, the police still don't have no leads on their murders. But I'm figuring—whoever did it—was after me."

When he said that, my head snapped back and my eyes bulged from their sockets. I was worried that once he figured out I was after him, he would flee and I would never be able to prove that he murdered my mother.

"Of course I considered that," he said into the phone. "I know my customers and I know my competitors. Neither would have come to my doorstep, first off, and neither would have killed my brother. They all knew my brother. This—this is something else. This is personal."

He knew. And that meant he was getting close. He would figure out that it had to be someone who hated him, and that would lead him back to me. I was running out of time, and that made me sweat.

"Nah," he continued, ending his pacing. "It wouldn't be them, neither. We settled our differences. The person that did this isn't that kind of enemy. This is someone who wants revenge. My neighbor said he heard the gunshots and saw someone running from the house when he looked out his window. Whoever it was, looked like a female."

I swallowed a lump in my throat, wincing, and shrinking away from the gap and the door. Someone saw me. That changed everything.

"Don't worry, I'll have it brewed and ready for you tonight," Leonard said to the person on the phone. "Talk to you then."

He headed back into the kitchen to hang up the phone.

I started fidgeting, twisting and turning my body and head as I looked for another escape route. The window was my single hope and chance to get the hell out of his room, but I hesitated to rush toward it. With the door open, I would be exposed. And I doubt if I had the strength in my good arm to lift the damn thing with the dirt and grime sealing it shut.

I needed another way out.

Fast.

I scanned my eyes across the room from corner to corner. He had two doors other doors in the bedroom. I figured one led to a closet and the other to a bathroom.

I was about to make my way toward the door closest to me, but I heard Leonard walking from the kitchen.

I scampered to hide myself behind the door again. I looked through the gap and he was coming straight for the bedroom. I held my breath.

A sudden knock at the front door stopped him in his tracks, and he turned to answer it. I let out my breath and held my hand over my heart.

"Who is it?" he shouted.

Outside, a familiar voice responded.

"Sorry to bother you, sir, I'm lost and need some directions."

It was Steve. He had come to my rescue.

I peered through the gap and watched as Leonard opened the door.

Steve was standing on the other side, grinning. He reached out to shake Leonard's hand. "How's it going?" Leonard ignored the gesture.

"Yeah?" Leonard said, folding his arms and gritting his teeth.

"Uh, yeah," Steve stuttered. "I took a wrong turn. I'm looking to get back onto the main road."

Leonard stepped outside, and he and Steve walked off the porch, out of view.

That was my chance, and I used it.

I scrambled for the door to the cellar, staying low.

I coursed my tracks through the cellar, making certain I didn't knock over or bump into any of Leonard's junk. I turned out the light and rushed for the cellar doors, hurrying up the concrete steps and fleeing toward a wired fence. I tried to climb over it, but tripped, falling into a pile of leaves on the other side.

It was difficult trying to be athletic with a cast on my arm. It slowed me down. But I managed to get to my feet and escape into the woods.

I had to take the long way around to get back to where Steve had parked his car. I pushed myself to run faster, trampling over the stiff leaves and twigs scattered by the wind across the ground.

I had no sense of direction.

Every footpath looked the same.

My instinct instructed me to head toward the sun hidden by clouds, and that's what I did. I ran until I came across a road. When I reached it, I checked both ways for traffic.

A car was speeding toward me from up the road. I didn't recognize it, at first. It was moving in a dust storm of dirt. But as it neared, I recognized the roar of the engine. It was Steve.

He must've been doing eighty or better. He drove past me, made a sharp U-turn, swerving back in my direction. He screeched to a halt inches away from me.

I ran around to the passenger's side and climbed in, closing the door and locking it.

"Go!" I shouted.

He slammed his foot on the gas and the car thundered forward.

"Thank you, Steve," I said to him. "That was a close call."

"I knew I had to do something when I saw him pull up to the house," he said.

"You saved my life," I said to him.

"I blew the horn first, but, when I realized that didn't work, I came up with a plan b."

"I'm glad you did."

"So what happened?" he asked. "Did you get what you were looking for?"

"No. He had the murder weapon on him."

"So now what?"

"I'm out of options, Steve," I said, rubbing my forehead. "By coming back to the past and changing circumstances and events, I upset crucial events."

"We know that already," Steve pointed out. "But what're you going to do?"

"I think Leonard knows it was me who shot his twin brother."

"How?"

"Leonard was on the phone telling someone that a neighbor saw a female running from the house the night that I shot his twin brother. Now I don't have the beer cans, the murder weapon, and that piece of shit is still a free man."

"And worse, the young sexy you has to walk around with the older, bitter and angry you for God knows how long," he added.

"Thanks, Steve," I said sarcastically.

"Wow. You really messed everything up, didn't you? You should never time travel without a qualified time travel agent planning out your itineraries."

I smirked. "Nice one. Very funny. I'll keep that in mind if there is a next time."

"When I reach your age, I'm going to find this guy, this hypnotist, and have him do to me what he did to you, so that when I end up back in time, I won't answer my door when you come knocking."

That made me grin. I loved Steve's sense of sarcasm.

"That Leonard guy is a real scary guy," he said. "I was shaking in my boots when I had to talk to him. I don't know, but he seemed suspicious. And worse, he knows my car now. So I'm in this with you,"

"Hopefully not," I said.

"So far everything that has gone wrong has gone wrong because you can't predict what's going to happen next. You only know what happened in your past—when you were—you know—the *sexy you*. But now you're not only reliving that past, you're altering it because you're doing more than reliving it. You're interacting with it. And I was never involved in any of this in the original chain of events. I was preparing for college. Enjoying rock and roll. Probably using this same car as a girl magnet. Now I'm driving around a murderess."

"You're right," I agreed. "But I know you're doing this because you care. You're a good person, Steve. That's why you came out here with me. That's why you believed me. That's why I told you the truth, knowing it would be difficult for you to believe. You're the only person I can trust with what I've told you. I can't let anyone else know. Especially, no one in my family. Least of all my baby brother. I can only imagine how crazy all of this sounds."

"Well, I guess it's more difficult for you," Steve said. "You lost your mom."

"Twice now."

"Yeah. I can't say I know what you're going through. I wouldn't know what to do if I lost my folks. So, I can't even imagine your pain."

"I can't really think about that right now," I said. "I have to stop Elroy Leonard…" I looked at him, scowling my brows in anger. "From existing."

He glanced at me, not knowing what to say. He knew I was serious and intent on ending the life of Elroy Leonard. He understood the reasoning behind my motivation. But I didn't know how to get him to understand my feelings—or how to justify them.

He looked away from me, continuing to drive in silence. After a moment passed, he looked in the rearview-mirror. His mouth fell open. He checked both side view mirrors and his face became as pale as a white sheet.

"Uh-oh. **Uh-oh**. Oh, no, no, no. I think that fucking guy's following us."

"What?"

I turned around in my seat to look through the back window. Leonard's truck was hot on our tail.

"Oh, shit. He followed you."

Steve looked at me in horror.

I returned the expression. "If he catches us, he's going to kill us."

CHAPTER NINETEEN

ELROY LEONARD HAD BOTH HANDS gripped tight on the steering wheel of his pickup truck as he sped up behind us. He moved in, similar to a shark closing in on its prey. He was intent on rear-ending us.

Through the windshield of his vehicle, I noticed his brows puckering into a sinister frown and his dark eyes narrow in madness.

I turned back to face Steve.

"Keep going," I told him. "Hit the gas."

Steve sweltered in fear, and he fidgeted in his seat. He put his foot on the gas pedal, pressing it down to the floor. His car went from fifty miles per hour to ninety in twenty seconds flat.

But Leonard was still on our tail, catching up.

"This guy is intent on killing us!" Steve freaked out. "Look, next time you're looking for an escort, call the cops!"

"Whatever you do, don't panic. Just keep driving. We can't let that bastard get on top of us."

"What the hell kind of engine does he have in that thing?" Steve asked.

I had no idea. I knew as much about cars as I knew about fighter jets. Zero. But what I did know was that if we didn't outrun him, he would ram us from the road the way he did my aunt's car. I wasn't going to let that happen. I knew how much Steve loved his car, and I didn't want to see anything happen to it or him.

"How good of a driver are you?" I asked him.

"What?" He didn't understand the question, and his breath burst in and out from terror. He hardly kept a steady grasp on the steering wheel.

I grabbed the wheel from him and turned it in my direction. The car swerved off the road and into the open plains.

"Keep your foot on the gas!" I ordered him.

"What're you doing?" he screamed. "We should've stayed on the road! His truck is more equipped for this kind of terrain. My vehicle is for the open road."

"I have a plan," I replied.

"Your plans never work out," he said. "That's why he's behind us right now trying to kill us!"

"We'll be okay if you just stay calm," I said to him, eyeing Leonard's vehicle from the mirror.

"He's gaining on us," Steve said in a shaky voice. His forehead dripped with perspiration.

"That's what I want," I said.

"What?"

"Trust me," I told him, keeping my eyes on Leonard's pickup truck. "Ease off the gas. Let him catch up to you?"

"Are you nuts?"

"Just do it, Steve!"

He did, and his car reduced speed. Leonard was gaining, beaming in victory, pounding his hand on his steering wheel, confident he had us. The closer his vehicle got to ours, the clearer I saw every muscle in his upper body flexing as he accelerated for the kill.

I had to plan our escape with perfect timing. Under my breath, I whispered a countdown, measuring the distance from his vehicle to ours. As he neared the bumper of Steve's car, I reacted.

"Okay, now! Turn right! Fast!"

Steve swerved right, and his car did a total one-eighty, skidding in a circle around Leonard's pickup truck and behind it.

Leonard had to slam on his brake, turn the wheel, as he tried to keep an eye on us. We chased each other in circles, our rear tires kicking up clouds of dust, throwing Leonard into a darkened smoke cloud of uncertainty. He wasn't able to see our movements. The trail of dirt and smoke blinded him.

Steve circled around the pickup three times before steering his car back toward the main road.

When we reached the road, Steve floored it. He pushed his hot rod to the limit of the speedometer. I kept my body twisted in my seat, facing the back, staring out the window, waiting to see Leonard's pickup truck.

It appeared in a dust cloud, veering onto the main road, coming after us. But we managed to gain a quarter mile distance—or, at least, a safe enough distance where it wasn't going to be easy for him to catch up to us.

But I had no time to relax. He was still determined to rear-end our vehicle to get to us.

We were fortunate that Steve had the faster vehicle in the long stretch.

As he kept peering from the road to the rearview, keeping the car at its top speed, I leaned forward in the seat, trying to figure out our location. I looked for landmarks and street signs. In the distance, I recognized an upcoming intersection and a billboard sign near it.

"Keep going straight," I said to Steve. "Head for that sign."

"Why?" he asked.

"I remember it," I responded. "Whenever my college friends and I were heading home from school, we would be speeding along that intersection. There's always a police cruiser there, waiting for reckless and speeding drivers. We were pulled over for speeding through that intersection several times. It was a game we played with the cops."

"I wish this was a game. One where I wasn't crapping in my pants."

"If we're lucky, there's a police car out there today. Keep your fingers crossed."

Steve crossed his right hand fingers while still holding the steering wheel. He was a mess of wrecked nerves, quivering and muttering to himself. "Come on… come on….come on," He kept his eyes on the road ahead, searching for any sign of a police cruiser.

I turned around in my seat, looking back at Leonard's truck. He was gaining. Steve's car wasn't as fast as I thought. Or Leonard had an engine under his hood made by aerospace engineers.

"He's gaining," I said.

Steve looked in his side-view mirror. "Damnit!" he exclaimed. "I can't go any faster!"

I turned around and placed my hands on the dashboard, looking straight ahead. We were nearing the intersection. I looked for any sign of a police cruiser. My eyes explored each direction of the crossroads.

As we roared into the meeting point of the roads, I had to make a fast decision.

"Go left!" I shouted.

Steve swerved the car in the that direction.

I eyed the area near the billboard. No police car. I tightened my fist in frustration. *Now what*? I asked myself.

The turn at the crossroads slowed our car down, and Steve had to stomp on the gas pedal to accelerate back to top speed.

Leonard turned into the intersection about a yard behind us. The turn was too sharp for his vehicle and it almost toppled over onto its side. But Leonard managed to win control over its weight and keep the vehicle on the road.

We had the advantage once again. Leonard's vehicle trailed behind us.

"We have to outrun him," I said to Steve.

"I'm so scared right now, I can get out and do that with my feet," Steve quipped back.

"He's falling behind," I said. "Keep going. Head for town."

Steve looked at his side-view mirror and I looked at the mirror on my side of the car, monitoring Leonard's vehicle, making sure we stayed ahead of him.

Neither of us noticed the police car that appeared up the road, traveling in the opposite direction.

We raced past it at an insane speed, and the cop at the wheel hit his brake. He swerved the police car around and accelerated after us with the siren blaring.

Steve and I looked at each other the moment we heard the siren. We didn't say a word. Our expressions said it all. We erupted into cheers and slapped each other's open palm.

"All right! That's what I'm talking about!" Steve shouted in celebration. "I have never been more happier about being pulled over by the police."

He pulled the car over to the side of the road and turned off the engine.

The cop must've been running our plate number because he didn't get out of his car right away. He was talking on his radio.

Steve and I sprang from his vehicle, waving our arms to get his attention. He got out of his car, one hand on the holster of his weapon. He started walking toward us.

We ran up to him, pointing in the direction of Leonard's truck. The cop ignored us, telling us to: "Stay where you are."

I kept pointing toward Leonard's truck as it neared, trying to get the cop to look. He kept his focus on us.

At that moment, Leonard stopped the pickup and turned around, heading back the way he had come.

"What are you doing?" Steve shouted to the cop. "He's getting away! That guy was trying to kill us! You need to go after him! He's deranged!"

"Just calm down," the cop responded. Never once looking back.

Leonard's pickup disappeared back up the road.

"It's hard to calm down after pissing your pants!" Steve bellowed. "That pickup was going to run us off the road! You need to stop him!"

The cop didn't allow Steve's rant to distract him from his duty. "I need to see ID," he said. "Do you have your driver's license with you? Your registration?"

Steve reached into the back pocket of his jeans and pulled out his wallet. "Yeah, yeah." He pulled out his license and registration and handed them to the cop, who looked them over.

I walked along the road, clenching my jaw and scrubbing my hands over my face in frustration.

Elroy Leonard got away again, and I wondered what I was going to have to do to end this cat and mouse game with him.

I threw my head to the sky and threw my hands in the air before turning to walk back toward Steve's car. The cop approached me holding his memo book.

"Miss... you're with him, right?" he asked.

"Yes, officer."

"And what's your name?"

"Anne. Anne Donovan."

"Donovan?"

"Yes."

He put his memo book into his back pocket and grasped his gun holster. "I need for you to come with me."

I looked at Steve. He made a face, shaking his head, more perplexed and stunned than I was.

My face drooped and I swallowed a lump in my throat, as I realized, by the look on the cop's face, he wasn't taking me in for being a passenger in a speeding vehicle. This was something far more serious.

CHAPTER TWENTY

THE POLICE RELEASED STEVE with a speeding ticket after questioning him, but they took me to the station and placed me in a square interrogation room no bigger than a prison cell.

I sat in a metal chair, tapping my fingers on a metal table, waiting to be interrogated. Or find out why I was being detained this time. I hoped it wasn't for the double murders, but I leveled my posture just in case it was. I wasn't going to say a word without an attorney present, and I had the upper hand because I knew the police didn't have the murder weapon. It was at the bottom of a lake.

After a few passing moments, Detective Kelly entered the room with a folder in his hand. He closed the door behind him, walked to the table and sat across from me in an empty folding chair.

I dignified my bearing by crossing my legs and raising my chin.

"Sorry we kept you in here so long, Anne," Detective Kelly said in a cordial tone. "I had to finish some paperwork."

"That's fine," I responded. "I'm just curious why I'm being detained."

"Detained?" He shook his head, making a face. "We're not detaining you, Anne."

"Then why am I here?"

"You were reported missing by your aunt. We also have a report that you disappeared from the hospital. It's usually policy that, if found, we bring you in for questioning. Unless you're in need of or request medical attention first. Standard procedure in adult cases."

I sighed. Relieved. "Is that it?"

"That's it," he responded.

"Well, as you can see, I'm okay."

"Why were you at Elroy Leonard's house?"

He caught me off guard, but I didn't break my stare. I sat in my chair unmoved and in control, quick to respond to his question. "I was near his house, driving around with my boyfriend."

"The young man you were pulled over with is your boyfriend?"

He seemed surprised. Steve didn't appear to be my type. I knew that was what he was thinking as he studied me.

I had to relax and convince him otherwise.

"Yes. I left the hospital to be with him. I'm in love with him. And he helps me get through rough times. He decided to take me out for a drive. Wind in my hair and face soothes me. It's a girl thing."

"I see. Why did you tell the officer Elroy Leonard was trying to kill you two by running your boyfriend's car off the road?"

"He was. He was chasing us."

"Okay, but why? Why was he chasing you?"

"I think he wants me dead because of what I told you. You went back and told him what I told you. So now he believes I'm out to get him. He's paranoid. And he has every right to be. He murdered my mother."

"We asked him some questions this morning at his house. We examined his vehicle for damage."

"And?"

"No damage."

"He must've repaired it," I said. "This guy works fast."

"He also had an alibi as to his whereabouts during your accident."

"So that's it? He gets away?"

"The investigation is ongoing."

"Detective Kelly, if he gets away…"

"Unless he confesses to a crime, we have nothing else to go on except your accusations."

"Is he a suspect, at least?"

"He's definitely a person of interest, but that's all I can share with you."

I grunted, gnawed my teeth.

"We contacted your aunt to let her know you're safe and sound," he said, getting up from the chair, and looking at his wrist watch. "She's on her way here to take you home."

"Can I leave now?" I asked him. "I want to see my boyfriend. Is he okay?"

"He's fine. He's waiting for you in the lobby."

I stood. "Am I free to go?"

"Sure. But don't you want to wait for your aunt?"

"I have to deal with my mother's murder in my own way, detective," I said to him. "I'll let my family know that I'm safe."

He nodded, opening the door and allowing me to go without another word. But I knew it wasn't going to be my last time seeing him. The look on his face told me that. I was no longer a teen who lost a loved one. I was a suspect.

I met Steve in the lobby and we rushed from the police station, heading to his parked car.

"Did you get a ticket?" I asked him.

"You know I did," he replied. "A hundred bucks. I just paid some cop's salary. What about you? Why did they detain you?"

"Nothing serious. I left the hospital without being discharged and my aunt filed a missing person's report. Did the police ask you any questions?"

"Like what?"

"About Leonard."

"Just why was I there with you at his house. Then they wanted to know what relationship I had with you."

"What did you tell them?"

"I told them to ask you about that."

I stopped, reaching for his hand with my good hand. "Look, Steve, I appreciate everything you've done for me, but maybe it's time for you to go home. It's not safe, and I don't want anything to happen to you. Leonard is coming after me now. I know he's capable of murder. That makes him dangerous. I don't have any choice but to face him. But you do have a choice. You have your whole life ahead of you. You have college and girls—you have a future. I might not have one at this point. I think it's time I face this alone."

He lowered his head, considering his options. He looked at me with sad, puppy-dog eyes. "Is that what you want?"

"I don't want anything to happen to you. I couldn't live with myself if anything did. You have too much to look forward to in your life."

"I mean, yeah, sure, I would hate for anything to happen to me, too," he said. "But I can't leave you now. I mean, you don't have a place to stay. You need food and stuff. You definitely need a bath."

I smiled. "You make me sound like a stray."

"No, I didn't mean it that way," he said. "I just want to help. I mean, you have no way of getting around. And you need someone there as a sort of lookout. Just in case."

"You're really sweet, Steve," I said, kissing him on the cheek. "And braver than I thought."

Steve blushed, putting his hands in his pants pockets. "Well, I won't say I'm brave. I—I just don't have many real friends. I'm kind of a loner. And I guess I want to see you get this guy for what he did."

"We'll talk about that some more later," I said. "But I need to call my aunt. Then I need to talk to my baby brother. My mother's funeral is today."

"Maybe you should go," he suggested.

"I've already been."

I turned away from him and walked toward his car, which was parked four or five cars down from the police station. As I reached the passenger side, I noticed Elroy Leonard's pickup truck parked across the street.

He sat in the driver's seat, his reflection emerging in the side-view mirror. He blew circles of smoke from a cigarette as he watched us. When he realized I spotted him, he grinned. He started the vehicle and drove off.

The muscles in my face tightened as he drove past me, smirking.

Steve came up behind me. "Was that him?" he asked.

I didn't remove my eyes from Leonard's vehicle. Glaring, I replied, "I had enough of Elroy Leonard."

Steve looked at me, knowing how much I wanted Leonard dead.

"What now?" he asked.

"I need a favor."

"Sure, anything."

"Can you drop me off someplace? I can't tell you what that place is—not yet—but I need to be there right now."

"Sure."

I turned around and walked to Steve's car, getting in. He climbed into the driver's seat and started the engine.

"Where to?" he asked.

"The elementary school playground."

"Uh-oh. I think I know where this favor is and what you're going to do."

CHAPTER TWENTY-ONE

WHEN STEVE AND I ARRIVED at the playground, we were overwhelmed by the smell of pot smoke and the stench of alcohol.

Crowds of teens hung out from one end of the playground to the other, listening to music, dancing, and making out. I remember hanging out with a few of them before going off to college. I used to think it was cool being wayward. But when I looked at them now, I saw them through the eyes of a woman in her fifties, and I wanted to call the cops on them.

I scowled as I made my way through them, rolling my eyes whenever they looked at me, shoving them whenever they bumped into me.

One of them, a boy high school age, offered me a rolled up marijuana joint, laughing. I snatched it from him, tossed it to the ground, and stepped on it. His mouth dropped open and he fell to his knees, grabbing his baseball cap and yanking it down on his head. He looked at me slapping his hands against his cheeks.

"What the hell you do that for?" he cried out.

"Don't you know there's a war on drugs from the current president in this time?"

He made a face, totally at a loss. "What?"

"You need to go home before I call Nancy Reagan on you."

Steve looked at me and said, "You sound like one of their teachers."

"Good, " I replied. "That's the benefit of being an adult. You learn more to teach more."

"Didn't you use to be like them when you were the age of the body you're in?" Steve said, scratching his head.

"That was a long time ago," I said.

"Wow. You really are a parent in that body," Steve quipped. "Do you even end up having any kids in the future?"

I didn't answer him.

I noticed that some of the teenagers in the playground had started staring at me.

Many of them knew who I was, others knew of me.

But they weren't looking at me because I was acting strange. They were looking at me because they knew my mother had been murdered.

Many of them seemed surprised to see me there, while others pitied me with distressed looks. Not one of them offered comfort or condolences.

When I stared back, some of them dropped their stares, while others went back to partying. They were too immature to know how to express grief for the girl whose mom had been murdered. If I had been their age, I would've reacted the same way.

Steve noticed their gazes and looked at me to see my reaction.

"You okay?" he asked.

"Of course," I responded.

"You sure you want to go through with this?" he asked.

"You know I do."

He shrugged. "I figured as much."

Steve knew I needed to find the person who every pothead and delinquent in town looked up to—the person who they relied on to feed their habits. And I knew where to look for him—thanks to memory.

He always hung out near the sandbox and seesaws. That was on the other side of the playground, closer to the school. We headed in that direction. I took the lead while Steve trailed behind me. The closer we got to where that person was, the more jittery Steve became. I heard him jingling his car keys and gritting his teeth.

I understood why he was fidgety. The person I had come to the playground to see was notorious for bullying guys who wouldn't fight him back. And he had a track record for run-ins with the law. Mainly misdemeanors. He was a rebel lowlife, but, unlike Elroy Leonard, he was no murderer.

I spotted him before Steve did. Scott Wozzack, better known as the Blitz. He wore skin-tight leather pants and a leather jacket with keychains of skulls dangling from the shoulders and pockets. His hair was dyed jet black and fluffed out to imitate an eighties rock star look. He sported a single skeleton earring in his right ear and diamond studs in his nose. Flashy for a two-bit delinquent who sold drugs and weapons as a full-time profession.

His three cronies had a handicap sense of style and flair than he did. They were outfitted more for high school classrooms than punk stardom, with baby faces that made them more of a ridicule than intimidating.

One of them jumped from the monkey bars to intercept me and Steve as we approached their crew.

I recognized him right away. His name was Bobby Jennings, a high school dropout who hung around Scott for protection from bullies who teased him about his weight. I remembered him from my youth. We called him Bunk and tormented him for being a mama's boy. Now he was in my face protruding his chest as if he was tough.

"Where do you think you're going?" he asked me and Steve, trying to augment more manliness in his otherwise squeaky voice.

"I need to see Scott," I answered him.

"For what?" he asked, holding his hand up to prevent us from moving past him.

"That's my business," I said, pushing him aside.

"Hey!"

I grabbed Steve by his arm and made my way toward Scott and his other two gofers.

When they saw us, they jumped up from the swings they sat on and blocked our path. I shoved my way through them, still holding Steve by the arm, and stomped over the rubber mat toward Scott.

He had headphones over his ears, listening to a cassette Walkman. I heard the song that was playing: *The Boys of Summer* by Don Henley.

He bobbed his head with his eyes closed, trying to sing the lyrics.

I tapped his shoulder and he opened his eyes, snatching the headphones from his ears.

"What the hell are you doing, Bimbette?" he snapped. "I'm listening to music!"

"We tried to stop her, Blitz," one of the cronies said from behind me.

Scott reached into his jacket pocket and pulled out a loose cigarette, putting it into his mouth. He pointed at me, nodding his head.

"I know you," he said. "Didn't your mother die or something like that?"

"My mother was murdered," I said, correcting him.

"You're Carol Donovan," he said, lighting his cigarette.

"Anne. It's *Anne* Donovan," I said, correcting him.

"What do you want?" he asked, blowing a circle of smoke from his mouth.

"I need a favor."

"I don't do favors," he retorted. "I do business. You looking to do business?"

I sighed. "You know I am if I'm here right now. The question is, *can* we do business?"

He shrugged. "That's up to you."

I shook my head, laughing to myself. "You don't have to play stupid with me. You and I both know you keep your stash of drugs buried in that sandbox over there. You also keep guns there, too."

"Who told you that?"

"Look, Scott—or Blitz—or whatever you want to be called—I need to buy a gun from you."

"Even if I had guns—which I don't—why would I sell you one? You never even buy bud from me. You're a goody two-shoes."

I sighed again, louder this time. "Okay, I get it, you have to be careful about who you deal with. I get that. But you know I used to hang out here and party just like the rest of you privileged morons. I bought drugs from you twice in the past. When I was seventeen. You probably don't remember because you smoke a lot of your own product."

Scott looked at Steve. "Who's the dweeb?" he asked.

"A friend," I answered him, without breaking my glare into his stoned red eyes. "He's cool. Now, can we do business or not?"

He hesitated, looking back and forth from me, to Steve, to his dorky friends and back to me. He nodded his consent and turned toward the sandbox, walking with a nonchalant stride in that direction.

I followed him, gesturing for Steve to stay where he was.

Scott kneeled onto both of his knees once he reached the sandbox and began digging his hands into the sand. After a moment, he pulled out a clear ziplock bag with a gun in it.

He dangled it in his hand for me to see.

I nodded my approval and walked toward him, taking the bag in my hand and opening it. I tossed the plastic bag aside and held the gun in my good hand, weighing it.

Scott looked at the cast around my hand. "I hope that's not the hand you shoot with," he said.

"I'm ambidextrous," I said to him.

He had no idea what that word meant. He stood there looking at me with this blank look on his face. I remembered that he never made it past the seventh grade and had a brain as hollow as wood. I knew I was going to have to explain it to him in layman terms.

"I can shoot just as well with either hand," I clarified.

When he understood what I was saying, he smirked, nodding his head.

"Oh. Okay. Cool."

I returned my attention to the revolver, gripping my hand around it to make sure it was a good fit for my hand size.

"Don't shoot yourself," he joked. His lame friends laughed with him.

I tightened my hand around the rubber grip. "I like it. The grip allows my index finger to easily reach the trigger without moving my palm away from the gun axis."

I lifted my arm and aimed the revolver in the direction of Scott's three followers. They dove to the ground.

"Good aim. Easy to stabilize for better precision and less recoil from holding it with just one hand. I like it."

Scott backed away from me. He was amazed by my knowledge of shooting a gun.

"Where did you learn—"

"—My father," I said, cutting him off. "What are you asking for it?"

"I can do three hundred," Scott replied.

"Two hundred," I shot back.

He thought about it for a moment. "That's highway robbery," he retorted.

"That's a fair price considering you're not a licensed gun shop dealer and we're negotiating illegal firearms with scratched off serial numbers in a children's playground."

"You got a point," he agreed.

I looked to Steve. "Give him the money."

He looked at me vacant, at first, before it registered to him what I had said. He snapped back into reality and reached into his pocket, pulling out the money and handing it to Scott.

As Scott counted the money with his two gofers, I put the revolver into the pocket of my jacket. "Are we good?"

Scott handed the money to one of his cronies and nodded. "Yeah. We're good."

"Thanks."

I started walking away, making sure Steve stayed with me. When we reached the end of the rubber mat, I stopped and turned around.

"Oh, and Blitz...."

He looked at me, hands in the back pockets of his tight leather pants.

"Six months from now, Melissa Anderson's father is going to find out that you've been messing around with his sixteen-year-old daughter and permanently reconstruct your face. Just thought you should know. You might want to consider finding someone of legal age."

He eyed me with a dumbfounded expression on his face, wondering how the hell did I know about him and Melissa Anderson.

"Take care," I added with a grin.

I walked off, heading back to the car with Steve.

When we made it back to the car, I climbed in removing the revolver from my pocket and examining it.

Steve got in and started the engine.

"Do you think you should have mentioned that about his future?"

"It doesn't matter. His future has jail written all over it no matter what," I responded.

Steve hit the gas and screeched away from the school playground.

"Okay, so what's next?" he asked.

"We go back to your place and remove this cast from my arm. Then I need to take a shower and get ready."

"For what?"

"Elroy Leonard."

Steve became silent. The thought of facing Elroy Leonard again frightened him.

"There's something I need to do first. Tonight."

He regarded me with a concerned stare. "What?"

"I need to see my brother. I need to talk to Andy. I destroyed my future. I have to make sure he still has one."

CHAPTER TWENTY-TWO

WHEN WE ARRIVED BACK AT STEVE'S parents' house, I made my way to the bathroom and stripped off my clothes in a frenzy, hurrying into the shower.

The moment I stepped onto the cold ceramic floor and turned the knob to the "on" position, I felt the water cleanse the silt of grime wedged to my skin. Within moments, the water boiled into a screen of steam that seeped into the sores and bruises of my wounds like an ointment.

With my good hand, I bathed the portions of my frame that had not been marred by Elroy Leonard's attempts to end my life. I stood with my head tilted to face the shower head and allowed the water to cascade over my body as if I was standing in a waterfall.

After a few moments, the creaking pipes and spattering drips on the ceramic floor became deafening. Only the thoughts in my head became audible.

I thought about Andy and what I was going to say to him when I saw him again. I thought about Elroy Leonard and confronting him again. I thought about my mother and how I failed her a second time.

At that moment, I wished I had never come back to the past. Or had tried to change it. Two innocent people would still be alive and Steve would be getting ready for college. My impulsive actions changed every circumstance around me, and, if I didn't set things right again, more innocent lives would be affected.

I shut my eyes, clearing my thoughts, swept away by the rapture and the nirvana the balmy water brought over my damaged body.

Before I knew it, ten minutes had become twenty until a knock came at the bathroom door.

"Are you okay in there?"

It was Steve.

I turned off the water. "I'll be right out."

"Okay," he answered. "I'm not trying to rush you or anything. It's just that my parents will be home in like another hour, and I wouldn't know how to explain a naked female neighbor in their shower."

"Okay. Almost done."

"My mom would freak out. My dad wouldn't, though."

"I understand. I'm just about done here. Just gotta dry myself off."

After moving to dry myself off and wrap a towel around my head, I slipped on a nightgown and robe Steve had left hanging on the back of the bathroom door. They belonged to his mother. They were a size too big. His mother wasn't petite.

I made my way down into the basement to Steve's bedroom. I was amazed by what I saw. His bed was dressed in fresh, new linen that was tucked in the corners. He had placed all of his dirty laundry in hampers, and the aroma of cologne he must've confiscated from his father, filled the air.

I sat on the chair at his desk and started sneezing. He walked over to me.

"Sounds like you're catching a cold," he said.

"Not exactly," I responded. "You laid on the Old Spice a little thick."

"Sorry about that."

"No worries," I smiled. "Are you ready to help me remove this cast?"

He nodded and walked over to his bed. He reached underneath it and pulled out something wrapped in a blanket, placing it on his bed. He unfolded the blanket and held large scissors in his hand.

"I borrowed this stuff from Mrs. Schumer around the corner," he said.

"I remember her," I reflected. "She was so nice."

"Was?"

"She passed away—"

"Don't tell me," Steve interrupted. "I don't want to know."

"She was a nurse, right? And her husband, a doctor?"

"These belong to her husband. She let me borrow them. She said these are what he uses to remove casts from patients."

"So let's get started." I placed my cast on his desk.

"Yeah, but, I don't know how to use these."

"Bring 'em here. I'll do it myself."

He brought the tools over and sat them on the desk.

"You sure you can do this?" he asked. "You might accidentally cut your arm off."

"In the future, we have what's called reality TV shows on cable television. I watched several medical shows. So, I think I should be fine."

I took the cast saw and began cutting into the plaster. Steve watched.

"Wow, what can't you do? You're good with guns, driving, removing casts. You're more macho than the Village People."

I laughed. "I guess I can't get any more macho than that."

I made two cuts onto the cast—one on the front of my arm, one on the back of my arm. I split the cast like a coconut with a cast spreader. I reached for the scissors and cut the padding. I felt a tickling sensation in my arm as I balled my bruised hand into a fist.

"Does it hurt?" Steve asked.

"It's still a little numb," I answered. "But I think I'll be able to handle a gun."

"Maybe you can use mental meditation to make the pain go away like they do in those karate movies."

"Actually, I've learned to trick my brain into not feeling pain. Pain is unavoidable, but, it only feels as bad as you want it to. It's basic psychology."

"My mom told me women can deal with pain better than men can because women bring babies into the world," Steve said.

"Your mom sounds like a smart woman."

Steve tossed the cast and padding into a trash bin near his bedroom door.

"So now what?" he asked.

"I can feel the fatigue in this body," I said to him. "It's as real as my mind wants it to be. I can feel every nerve and every aching muscle."

"Would aspirin help?" he asked.

"It might."

"Warm tea might help, too. My mom says warm tea relaxes her."

"I probably just need to rest for a few hours. Only if I could."

"You should try."

I hopped up from the bed. "No. I can't. I need to see my baby brother and I have to see him tonight."

"Why tonight?"

I stopped in the doorway, sighing, running my hands through my hair and trying to put a handle on my emotions. I didn't want Steve to see my anxiety. But my emotions were difficult to hide. My eyes scanned the thin air for a moment.

"In the other timeline, after my mother's funeral, my aunt moves us into her house. Then she sells our house. If I'm right, this is Andy's last night in our old house. He will move into my aunt's house tomorrow evening. If my being here hasn't changed or doesn't change what happens after the funeral. But it probably has already."

I paced the floor of Steve's bedroom, breathing in frustration. I was pissed at myself for lousing up my past. And maybe Andy's, too. Pissed that I had to now face Elroy Leonard alone.

"I was with Andy the entire time after my mother's death. I was there with him, at our house, the night before we moved into my aunt's house. But, in this timeline, I'm not. I'm here with you. So, something might have changed. I was supposed to be at my mother's funeral this morning. But I wasn't. For all I know, the police are probably out looking for me as a missing person again. I don't know. I changed so many events of the past, I don't know what's what or what happens next. That's why I need to see my brother."

I walked toward the bedroom door. Steve followed me.

"Where are you going?" he asked.

"Are my clothes ready?"

"They're washed," he replied. "I put them in the dryer a half hour ago. I'll go check and see if they've dried yet."

"Bring them to me in the bathroom upstairs." I rushed toward the stairs. "I have to hurry."

"Can I ask you something? What's it like?"

I made a face, not understanding the question.

"I mean, you lost your mom," he said, clearing his throat. "Not to a disease or accident or anything, but some guy who's clearly unhinged. It must really hurt. I mean, inside."

I didn't know how to answer him. How do you put those emotions in words? I leaned my back against the wall and searched my memories for the emotions I felt that fateful night. I didn't want to revisit that trauma in my life again, but I owed it to Steve to give him a straight answer.

"I would never want you or anyone else to experience what I had to go through," I responded, looking down, remembering everything Elroy Leonard stole from me.

"Hey, look, I'm sorry, I shouldn't have asked," Steve said walking toward me. "My dumb curiosity. You don't have to tell me."

"No," I said, making steady eye contact with him. "It's all right. You should know. People don't like to talk about these things. We keep them locked away inside of us. That's because it's too painful to discuss. But there's nothing worse than losing a loved one. And losing that special person is worse when you find out the reasons why."

I had to stop myself for a moment to fight the anger swelling in my soul.

"Death hurts. It leaves a void that you will have with you until the day you die. But murder… murder leaves scars that can never be healed. Not even over time."

I wiped my eyes and took a deep breath, composing myself. "It took me several years before I could even talk about the murder of my mother. Except to my therapist. Then I met a man—a very rich man—who had a heart of gold. He helped me through the roughest times. He nurtured me through it. He supported every effort I made to overcome the memories. If it wasn't for him, I would've never been able to afford to travel back in time through hypnosis. I would've never been able to hold on a long as I did without ending up in a mental institution like my baby brother."

"Good thing you met that guy, huh?" Steve said with a warm smile.

"Yes. It was. I don't know what I would have done without him."

"What happened to him?" Steve asked.

"I ended up marrying him," I replied, smiling.

Steve looked at me, smiling back. His look turned to concern when he noticed my sudden pensive gaze toward the ceiling.

"He's out there somewhere," I whispered. "In another part of the world. Living his life. And I may never see him again."

"You don't know that," Steve said, upbeat. "You know who he is and where he is and when and where you guys will meet someday. If you don't make it back into the future—into your old self—then you can still go out there and find him."

I snapped out of my pensive trance and looked at Steve. Once again, he managed to make me smile. "You're right. Maybe some good can come out of this. If I don't make it back into my future body."

"See, there you go. Just think positive."

"I better hurry," I said, still smiling. I started to walk off, but stopped and looked back at Steve over my shoulder. "You know, I don't believe a word of what I just said. There's no way this ends on a positive note."

I walked off, leaving Steve at a loss.

CHAPTER TWENTY-THREE

I GOT DRESSED AND HEADED out the basement door of Steve's house. He stayed behind, waiting for his parents, who would be arriving home soon. As I made my way outside, walking from the backyard to the front of the house, he appeared inside, moving from window to window, keeping an eye on me to make sure I was safe.

I walked along the sidewalk with my hands in my jacket pockets, jiggling my house keys in one pocket and gripping the handle of the gun in the other. The closer I got to the house, the more my steps became slow and hesitant. I wanted to turn around and go back to Steve's house. Not out of fear, but out of heartbreak.

As I neared my old house, I noticed that it was dark. No porch lights. No indoor lights. And the foundation itself squeaked in the wind. The aura of the house was eerie and ominous. It seemed as if the house itself lost its life the day my mother was murdered. The vivacity, the warmth, that made it my home was gone.

I stopped to take a deep breath at the curb, taking a moment to grapple with my emotions. I stepped off the curb and hurried across the street, checking both directions to make sure no cars were coming.

I pulled out the keys in my jacket pocket as I made my way to the porch, but something told me to stop and look around. I had this weird feeling that someone was out there in the dark, watching me. I gripped the handle of the gun in my pocket tighter, placing my finger on the trigger, preparing myself for whatever came next or whatever was waiting for me out there.

After a few moments of looking around, I made my way to the house and to the porch. I decided to go around to the back and enter through the rear door instead of the front.

When I entered the house, I found myself roaming around the kitchen, touching dishes still in the sink, caressing dish cloths and aprons that still carried my mother's scent.

I was amazed by how real and alive my senses were, considering I was reliving the past in hypnotic memory. Everything felt tangible and material. I was able to breathe the past into my senses.

I started making my way to the living room. Moving boxes cluttered the hallways and dining area. My aunt and uncle had moved out nearly all of the furniture except for one chair—a recliner—the chair my mother sat in whenever she watched television or hemmed fabric. She valued that chair more than any of her material possessions.

I walked toward it, rubbing my fingertips across the back, absorbing the feeling of the soft Serofoam, remembering how I liked sitting in the chair as a young girl. The memories brought a tear to my eye.

The nostalgic moment didn't last. High beams of light from a car outside pulling into the driveway seized my attention.

My aunt and uncle had arrived home with Andy, and that meant I had to get myself primed for the conversation I needed to have with him.

I rushed toward the stairs and hurried upstairs to his bedroom. I made my way into his room, hiding behind the door. I slid down the wall and waited.

I heard them enter the house. Their movements were lagged. I heard them walk from the foyer to the living room. No words between them. I heard the squeak of the closet door in the foyer opening and the sound of jackets being unzipped and placed on hangers. Sighs from my aunt echoed throughout the house as the lights came on downstairs.

I felt their grief as if it was my own. The silence of their mourning was still loud to my ears. They didn't need words.

I wanted to go downstairs and embrace them, but I wasn't prepared to answer the questions I knew they had. I wasn't here as that nineteen-year-old teenager. I was here as a middle-aged woman who was reliving the past.

I waited for Andy to come upstairs, but he didn't come straight to his bedroom. He went to the bathroom. I heard my aunt and uncle talking to each other downstairs, but their voices were muffled. Somehow, I knew it was about me. I knew they had to be worried about where I was and why I didn't show up at the funeral. But it was too dangerous to reveal myself to them.

I squirmed behind the door as I waited for Andy. My legs began to stiffen from the uncomfortable position. After a moment, I had to stand and rub my knees. That was when Andy walked through the bedroom door.

I immediately shut the door behind him and locked it.

He turned to face me, and I held my finger to my mouth, hushing him before he made a sound.

I placed my ear against the door to make sure my aunt and uncle were still downstairs. I heard them talking. It was safe to talk to Andy. I rushed over to him and hugged him. When I let him go, I saw the sour face he made. He was upset with me.

"How come you didn't come to mom's funeral?"

I heard the despondency in his tone. I held him by his shoulders and looked into his eyes.

"I was there, Andy."

"I didn't see you."

"I can't explain this to you now, Andy, but believe me when I tell you, I was right there with you. Feeling what you felt. Holding your hand. Crying your tears. I already lived it with you."

"What're you talking about? You weren't there. I would have seen you. You weren't there holding my hand. Why didn't you come?"

I knew he didn't understand. I couldn't explain it without telling him the entire truth. I would have to reveal that I was from the future and trapped in the body of my younger self. He wouldn't believe me. He would think I was making stuff up to pardon myself from not being at our mother's funeral.

I let go of him and walked over to his bed, sitting down.

"I know how you feel, Andy," I said, staring toward his bedroom window, looking at the things he was into—his baseball posters and trophies. "I know you're feeling nothing but anger, bitterness, and resentment. I didn't know then, but I know now."

He looked at me, his face creased as if he had something tart in his mouth.

"I neglected you before because I was dealing with my own anger and grief," I said to him. "But I won't make that mistake again. I won't fail you twice like I did with our mother. I won't let you live in isolated rage and resentment. I need you now more than ever."

"I don't know what you mean," he said.

I walked over to him. "I'm going to make sure no one harms our family ever again."

I held him by his shoulders again, kneeling before him, staring into his saddened eyes.

"I won't let Elroy Leonard take my family away from me again. But I can't do this unless you promise me that you will be strong. I need for you to be strong. You have to go to school. You have to pursue your dreams. You have to be there for me. I am going to need you in the future, Andy. I need you now. Promise me you'll do everything you need to do to reach your goals. Promise me that you won't shut down. That you won't let what that man did to our mother consume you with rage and hate. Promise me, Andy."

He looked at me, watery tears reflective in his eyes. "I promise," he said. "But what does Elroy have to do with mommy dying?"

That's right, I thought. *He didn't know.* In the original timeline, Elroy Leonard was arrested and convicted of killing our mother before Andy shot him to death. But now, Elroy Leonard was a free man. Thanks to me, he hadn't been arrested or convicted yet.

But how would I explain that to Andy? I was here to keep him safe and to protect him from the truth. I had to keep him from the rage and bitterness that drove him to murder Elroy Leonard outside that courthouse.

I stepped away from him, rubbing my hands.

"It's nothing, Andy. Forget about Elroy Leonard. Just listen to me. Finish school. Do what you can to help people. Respect women. Make friends. You will always need true friends. And most of all, don't ever shut down and withdraw from the world. Ever. Promise me that."

"I promise," he replied.

I walked to him and hugged him again, tighter and longer this time, kissing him on the cheek. He hated that, wiping the wetness from his cheek with the sleeve of his shirt.

"Yuck, sis," he complained. "That's not necessary."

"I don't care," I said. "It's my way of letting you know how much I love you."

"I know already," he sighed.

"No, Andy, you don't," I said with a whisper. "You're my only brother. You and I are all that's left of our mother. She would want us to be strong and stay close. That's why I need for you to be strong. I need for you to live."

He sighed again as he sat on his bed. "Okay."

I motioned toward the bedroom door, unlocking it. "I'm going to need your help in getting out of here. I can't let Aunt Sharon and Uncle Owen know I'm here."

"Where are you going now?" he asked. "You're not going to help us pack?"

"Not this time," I replied.

Andy wondered what I meant. My response made no sense to him. He stood there looking at me with a blank expression. But I looked away from him, going to the bedroom door and peeking out into the hallway.

"I have to make things better, Andy. That's why I have to go."

I turned to look back at him. He lowered his head, heaving a sigh.

"I need for you to go downstairs and make up some story to get Aunt Sharon and Uncle Owen out of the house. Tell them you need to go to Mr. Cohen's convenience store for stuff you need for a school trip. Make up something. Can you do that for me?"

He groaned, bouncing from his bed. "Yeah, all right."

As he walked to the door, I grabbed him again and hugged him.

"You mean everything to me, Andy," I said. "I'm going to see you again soon. Okay?"

"Okay," he answered.

"I just have to fix some things that went wrong. I'll be back. I'll be here for you this time. I'll make sure you grow up to live the life you were meant to live. The life our mother would've wanted for you. The life I want for you. I just need for you to focus on your future. I have to leave so I can protect you and Aunt Sharon and Uncle Owen. I have to protect you guys."

"From what?" he asked.

"I can't explain it to you now," I said as I opened the door to let him out. "But I will soon. Someday. I promise."

"Whatever," he replied.

As he walked out the room and into the hallway, I grabbed his shirt.

"Love you, Andy,"

"Yeah, me, too," he said.

I watched as he made his way toward the staircase and down the steps. I heard him talking to my uncle, telling him he needed to go to the convenience store. I heard my uncle yell to my aunt.

"Sharon, I'm taking Andy to the store real quick. Do you need anything?"

"No," I heard her answer. "I'll stay here and finish up on some packing. I have to go upstairs first."

Uh-oh, I thought, my eyes wide and heart in my throat as her foot started up the first step with a loud squeak. Andy stopped her, calling to her before she could take another step.

"Aunt Sharon! Come with us. I need your help in picking out the things I am going to need for my new school since we're moving."

"Okay, Andy."

She moved away from the stairs, and I let out my breath. I listened as the three of them made their way to the closet in the foyer to put their coats on. They headed out the house, closing the front door with a loud slam.

I waited for several moments before moving an inch. When I heard the engine of the car start in the driveway, I made my move.

I hurried down the steps and ran through the house, heading toward the kitchen. I rushed out into the backyard, making my way to the front of the house. The car was gone. I watched the taillights head up the street. I started to make my way back toward Steve's house when I noticed a pickup truck parked across the street. Even though it was dark, I recognized the model. It was Elroy Leonard's.

I placed my hand in my jacket pocket and clenched it around the butt of my gun. But I didn't see Elroy Leonard inside the vehicle. That made me nervous. I pulled the gun halfway out of my pocket, looking around.

Leonard appeared, coming out from behind a tree, zippering his jeans. He looked in my direction and grinned. He got into his pickup and started the engine.

He was fucking with me, and he knew it. But what he didn't know was that I wasn't afraid. I could've ended his life right there. I was a good shot. All I had to do was take the gun, aim it and it would be over.

My hand was itching to remove the gun all the way from my pocket and take aim. But my other hand reached over and clasped around my wrist, preventing me from doing it.

I eyed Leonard as he pulled out and drove toward me, slowing down to make sure I saw the sinister smirk on his face. He hit the gas and sped up the street, tires screeching.

He wanted me to know that he was targeting me and my family.

That meant, I was going to have to kill him sooner than I had planned.

CHAPTER TWENTY-FOUR

STEVE AND I HAD NO IDEA where we were.

We woke before dawn to begin our travel to find the house where the young Professor Singh lived. I had to depend on the old fashion way of directions—a Rand McNally road map. Steve knew more about reading print maps than I did, but he was too busy driving and tuning to radio stations. It felt weird listening to music that was new to him, but classics to me.

About an hour into our drive, as the dawn's light washed the horizon in blended tones of flushing pinks and pastel yellows, Steve pulled his car over to the side of the road. We needed to make sure Elroy Leonard wasn't following us. He checked the mirrors while I placed the gun in my lap.

"You nervous?" I asked him.

"Of course I am," he responded, his eyes exploring everything around him. "That nut case can be anywhere out there. And what's worse, we're lost."

"I know," I sighed. "I can't read this damn map. I'm used to digital mapping systems and GPS devices. These gas station road maps are outdated in my time."

"I have no idea what you're talking about. What's a GPS?"

"It's like a satellite tracking system that pinpoints your location and lets you know how far you are from your destination. Or something like that. I'm not a tech girl, but, in the future, you'll have cell phones and computers that help you find anything or anyone in the world."

"Wow. That sounds super cool. I'm looking more and more forward to the future every day. I just hope I end up actually seeing it someday."

"So do I."

He hurled a startled look in my direction, his mouth dropped open. He must've thought I directed my comment toward him. I placed my hand on his shoulder, reassuring him that it wasn't. "Oh, no. What I meant was a future for myself. Seeing the future once I'm back in my future body."

He nodded with a comforting smile. "You will." After a moment, he reached for the map. "Let me see that." He took the map and scanned through it as if he was perusing through a complex textbook.

I got out the car to stretch my legs and take in the countryside view. I inhaled the brisk morning air as my eyes engrossed upon the distant hills and wide open country. I had never seen a sight as beautiful and as serene as the landscape before my eyes. It was a panorama view natured with crop growing pastures and many-hued flowers—a smell of leafy plants that I breathed into my lungs with a long inhale. I shut my eyes as I breathed it all in.

At that moment, I wanted to be somewhere else. Some place where my reality was filled with green meadows and blue creeks. Some place where I didn't have to fret the past or the future. A place where I would be with both my brother and my mother. A place where no harm would ever come to us, and we would be happy. I saw that place in my mind, as I stood out in the middle of the long grass blowing in the wind, keeping my eyes closed and my nostrils open to the aroma of the fresh morning dew.

But the sudden sound of Steve honking the horn snapped me out of my trance, and I opened my eyes.

"Hey!" he yelled from the car. "Found it!"

I hesitated, not wanting to abandon my musing fantasies of a better world.

"What are you doing over there?" he asked. "Please don't tell me you have to pee."

I turned and headed back to the car, letting go of my fancies with a heaving sigh.

"No, I don't have to release myself. I have more class than to pee out in the open." I got in the car and closed the door. "Where do we have to go?"

"We're looking at doing some serious driving," Steve responded. "He's three hours away from here."

"We can take turns at the wheel," I said.

"I'm not worried about the driving part," Steve said. "I hope you brought money for gas."

With that, he started the car and put it in drive, hitting the gas pedal.

I didn't rest my eyes the entire time we spent on the road. I kept them peeled for Professor Singh's house and for any sign of Elroy Leonard.

When we reached the neighborhood where Professor Singh had his childhood home, the sun had settled into the horizon. The brisk November climate had mustered an aberrant chill in the air that settled over the entire suburb. I had the window down and felt the biting cold through my clothes.

Steve and I recognized Singh's childhood home right away. It sat in the middle of an opulent community—a palace with Mughal-style arches, pinked-hued columns and a grand entrance facing east. The courtyard was a decorated display of intricate latticework and calligraphy traditional of Indian architecture. It was a lavish home, to say the least.

Steve drove along the courtyard agape and shaking his head, impressed by the extravagant structure.

"Wow," he muttered. "This place is palatial. I'd never seen anything like it. The Singh family must be wealthy."

"If you saw the price tag on his hypnotic therapy session in the future, you'd know why," I said as the car came to a stop.

"You want me to wait for you in the car?" Steve asked.

"No," I answered. "I'd prefer you come with me. I need you by my side."

"You sure?"

"Of course I am. We do this together or not at all. You're a fast thinker, and I need that."

He looked at me, suddenly horrified.

"What's wrong?" I asked him.

"I just had a terrible thought," he said. "What if the young Singh sends the middle-aged you back to the future and the young, gorgeous you wakes up and sees me? She's not going to know what happened or who I am."

"We don't know what's going to happen until we get in there and talk to Professor Singh."

"I wish there was a way you could let the young you know what a great guy I am."

"I doubt if our consciousness will cross paths during transference for me to put in a good word for you."

I got out the car as Steve turned off the engine and got out after me. We made our way to the front entrance of the house.

Sprawling gardens and exquisite sculptures lined the winding path embellished with precious stones. The mansion, palace itself stood flanked by rows of lush trees swaying slightly in the frigid autumn breeze.

At its threshold stood a sandstone water fountain, its clear water pleasant sounding as it resonated in the cool air. When we reached the doorway, it took me a moment to find the doorbell. Before I did, Steve moved ahead of me and knocked on the palatial brass door.

After a few moments, a woman answered. Singh's mother. They had the same straight nose shapes and dark eyes. She wore a long skirt with a dupatta scarf, and brandished a vermilion mark on her forehead. She had to be no older than thirty-five, which meant she was a teenage girl when she was pregnant with Professor Singh.

She was still an attractive woman for her age, but she carried heavy bags under her eyes—either from aging or sadness.

She stuck her head out the partially opened door, staring at Steve and me as if we were there to sell her something. She gazed at us with an automatic distrust, openly staring at us with a raised brow. It was several seconds before she opened her mouth to speak.

"May I help you with something?"

Steve looked at me, waiting for me to say something. I cleared my throat, extending my hand. "Hi, my name is Anne Weather—" she looked at my hand as if offering a handshake offended her. "---excuse me—Anne Donovan. My name is Anne Donovan." I returned my hand to my jacket pocket. "I was wondering if your son was home."

"What do you want with him?" she asked, her tone of voice rigid.

"We go to the same school," I lied. "We just need to see him about an urgent matter. It's dealing with school."

Her suspicious eyes bore into me, probing me from top to bottom. She shifted to Steve, examining him. After a moment, she opened the door all the way to allow us entry.

"Is he expecting you?" she asked.

"No, ma'am," Steve responded.

"But we drove a long way," I interjected. "It's vital that we talk to him."

She nodded, and we followed her into the house. She led us to the living room area, gesturing for us to take a seat on a sofa with printed blue cushions. Everything from the paint to the carpet to the curtains had deep tawny reds and burnished oranges that gave the room an intimate warmth.

As Singh's mother left to go get him, I walked around the room, exploring the carved wooden details in the furniture and array of Indian prints in the décor. The fragrance of sandalwood infiltrated my nostrils. The scent of jasmine flower garlands left a trail in the air from the hair of Singh's mother. I heard the faint sound of someone playing a sitar from another room in the mansion. I presumed it was young Professor Singh because it stopped the moment I heard his mother call out his name.

"Arjun!" she shouted.

I heard her voice mumbling something to him.

Afterwards, I heard his footsteps heading to the living room. He appeared in the archway. I almost laughed when I saw him. He wore thick glasses and striped pants that came above his ankles. He stood tall and lanky, nothing similar to the future Professor Singh, who was more wiry and toned with middle-age stubble on his face and masculinity in his bearing. The young Singh, who stood before me now, had none of those attributes. Everything about him screamed nerd.

"Uh, hi, my, uh, mother said you were here to see me..."

Even his squeaky voice exposed a socially bungling person.

"She said you're from my school," he went on. "I don't think I've ever seen you around my school before."

I looked at Steve. He shrugged, at a loss. I stepped forward, approaching the young Professor Singh.

"No, you haven't seen us around," I said to him.

"So how is it that you know me?" he asked.

"We don't. Not yet."

He remained silent, casting confused looks at both me and Steve.

"You and I don't meet until another thirty-six years from now," I said to him.

He looked at me and made a face. "Is this a joke?"

"I wish it were. I really do. But it's not. My name is Anne Weatherford. That's my married name. In this time, I'm Anne Donovan. But I'm not from this time, Professor Singh."

"Professor..." he looked at Steve, then back at me.

"That's what you are... who... you are... who you become. In the future, some years from now, you're going to launch a hypnosis practice that transports people through time. I am one of your patients."

He stood gawking at me, not knowing what to say or how to respond. He still thought this was a joke.

"You're going to develop the ability to transfer a person's soul and consciousness back in time," I said to him. "This is no joke. Right now, my future mind and essence are trapped in my teenage body. I know that sounds crazy, but I'm telling you the truth. It's real."

He stuttered, but wasn't able to get out the words. He shook his head in disbelief.

"I'm telling you the truth, Professor," I grabbed him by the shoulders. "I know it seems impossible, but I am trapped here in the past in my teenage body and I need your help to get back to my future self. Please, Professor."

He gazed straight into my eyes as the shock of what I was telling him settled in. He had no reason to believe me. I knew that. But he knew, by the return gaze I gave him, that I was telling him the truth. After a moment of no reaction, no response, he beamed with joy.

"I can't believe it," he muttered to himself. "I cannot believe it! Grandfather was right!"

"What?" Now I was confused.

"If what you're telling me is the truth, then it means that my grandfather can really send people's consciousness through space and time. It means it's all real and I will someday be his successor."

"What do you mean someday?" I frowned.

"My grandfather's been teaching me how to use hypnosis since I was eight, but I don't have the gift, nor the abilities he has to actually send a person's memory and consciousness through time. I still have a long way to go to reach his level. But knowing that someday I will! There are no words to describe how happy that makes me."

He noticed my head drop and realized I didn't share his enthusiasm.

"Oh… wait… I didn't realize… you came here thinking I had the same abilities now that I will someday have?"

"Yes," I sighed.

"I'm really sorry."

"It's not your fault."

"Even if I did have the capabilities to use hypnotic transference, there would still be no way I could help you."

"What do you mean? The future you was the one who told me to come look for the younger you in this time."

"He did? I mean, I did. I don't know why."

"You must have some natural abilities to do what you do—even in this time."

"Well, you see, the way it works—and I learned this from my grandfather—once the transference is lost between the hypnotist and the patient under hypnosis, then there's no way to send that patient's soul or essence or consciousness back to its future self. Your memories and soul will become trapped in the past, and your future self—your future body becomes a mindless, soulless shell—devoid of its consciousness and spirit. You… you will… die in the future. That body dies. "

I stumbled back toward Steve. "There has to be some way."

"I wish it was possible," young Singh responded. "But it's like a telephone call. The hypnotist makes the call—into your mind and consciousness. You answer the call, then you decide to hang up. The hypnotist is still on the other line because he hasn't ended the call. He's still talking, still trying to reach you, but you won't answer because you ended the call. But if you were to pick the receiver back up, the hypnotist would still be there because he hasn't hung up. But if you don't pick up the receiver and the hypnotist doesn't hear you on the other end, then he hangs up the phone and ends the call completely. You can try dialing him back, but he's no longer there to answer the call. Do you get what I'm telling you?"

"Not really, no."

"Once you severed the connection between yourself and the future me, you ended communication. The line is dead now. You can't go back to your future self because my future self no longer has a direct line to bring your essence and consciousness back into the future."

I stood there a moment gawking at the young Professor Singh. I turned away and moved toward the sofa, plopping down into it with a sigh. I ran my fingers through my hair, burying my face into the palm of my hands.

Steve walked over and sat next to me. "Sorry, Anne," he said.

I lifted my head and laughed to myself. "I did this to myself."

"There's still another way," Singh said.

Steve and I looked at him as he stood there contemplating possibilities.

"You can still be transported—your consciousness, that is—just not back to your future body. But, it is possible to transfer your essence and mind back to the past."

I stood to my feet. "You mean, I can go back to an even younger age and earlier time than this one?"

"Yes."

I looked at Steve. "Then I can go back to my seventeenth birthday. Back to a time before any of this even happens. I can prevent my mother from ever meeting Elroy Leonard."

"How?" Steve asked me.

"I can keep them from meeting by preventing the circumstances that led to them meeting for the first time," I answered. I did not hide my excitement. "I can prevent myself from going through any of this."

"It sounds too good to be true," Steve said. "How do you know you won't screw things up again?"

"He's right," the young Professor Singh cut in. "You would still have the same awareness of the future as you have now. All of your memories and knowledge of things that has already happened. You know things about the future that we don't. Like who will become the next president or if there will be stock market crashes. Who you marry or divorce. You could damage your own future and that of others. As you have done in the current time. I shouldn't even be talking to you right now. It's dangerous."

"How?" I asked.

"Well, like now, for example," he replied. "I didn't know I would one day fill my grandfather's shoes and fully develop the ability of hypnotic transference until you told me. That may have inadvertently changed something in my own future."

"She has a tendency to do that," Steve said with a smirk.

I cut a stern look at him.

"Sorry," he said, lowering his head.

"Can you do it?" I asked Singh. "Can you send me back in time—again?

"I can't," Singh replied. "I wish that I could, but I don't know how."

My shoulders dropped, and I shook my head, frustrated and disappointed. I let out a breath and smacked my hand against my thigh.

"I can't do it, but I know that my grandfather can."

I perked up again. "You sure?"

He nodded a yes. "He can definitely do it."

"When?" I asked.

"I can send for him."

"Send for him?"

"Yes. He's in India."

"How long?"

"A day or two."

That wasn't good enough for me. "I don't have a day or two. I'm already out of time."

"What do you mean?" he asked.

"I'm facing a complicated dilemma," I responded.

"It's going to take my grandfather some time to travel from India to the States," Singh said. "He has to make travel plans, tickets, packing. Not unless you can travel to him."

"I can't afford it. Too expensive. And I don't have a passport in this time. I didn't get a passport until my twenty-seventh birthday."

Steve looked at me. "What do you wanna do?"

"What can I do?" I said, trying not to snap at him. "I have limited options."

"Well, whatever you do, I have your back," he said.

I smiled, and he smiled back. I reached over and rubbed his shoulder. "Thanks, Steve."

I walked toward the living room window and stared out, considering my options. I didn't have two days. I knew that. Elroy Leonard was scheming, and I knew he was going to make a move against me soon. Maybe even against my family. I had him worried and nervous, and that made him more dangerous and more of a threat.

He would kill me, Steve, Andy, and my aunt and uncle to keep from going to jail.

I looked back at the young Professor Singh and nodded to him.

"Call your grandfather," I said. "When he gets here, call me right away."

Young Singh nodded, then left the living room to make the call.

Steve approached me, his brows woven in a grimace.

"What are you going to do?" he asked in a whisper.

I shifted my body to face him. "Go through with my plan," I said in an icy tone. "I'm going to stop Elroy Leonard before he harms me or my family."

"Then what?"

"Then I go back in time to keep any of this from ever happening."

"What if you fail… and Leonard succeeds?"

For that, I had no answer.

CHAPTER TWENTY-FIVE

WHEN SINGH RETURNED TO the living room, he handed me a piece of paper that had his home telephone number written on it.

"Take this," he said. "Call me to let me know when you are on your way. My grandfather is taking the first flight out. He should arrive here by morning."

"I'll be back here the moment he arrives," I promised him.

We nodded to each other.

"I wish you good fortune until then," he said.

I looked at him, feigning a lackluster smile. I didn't feel optimistic. I knew the odds were against me. And even though I was nervous about facing those odds, I put on a façade of bravery.

I looked toward Steve for encouragement, and he acknowledged my look with a grin.

"You ready to go?" I asked him. He nodded.

"Let me see you out," Singh said, starting toward the foyer. He stopped short and looked back at me. "There is something else.

When I was talking to my grandfather on the phone just now, he told me something I did not know."

I looked at him with darting eyes, waiting to hear some bad news.

"There may still be a chance for you to return to your future self," he said.

I looked at Steve, my eyes widening from elation. I turned to face Singh again. "How?"

"You disconnected yourself from my future self the moment you allowed your memories, consciousness and essence to interact with the past. You refused to let go of the past and, by reliving it, you severed the hypnotic connection. Your mind did this. A hypnotherapist can only stay connected to an active mind for a short period of time. Once that time frame ends, the hypnotherapist has no choice but to remove himself from your thoughts and consciousness. He can always try to reconnect with your consciousness at some other point in time. Mainly, because your mind is still alive. It just needs to be transferred back to your original body. In your future time."

"What are you saying?" I asked. "I can be sent back to my future self if my mind allows it?"

"Yes."

"How?"

"You must go under hypnosis again, be put into a trance, and allow your memories to move forward. This opens the gateway and allows your mind passage through and into time. But my future self would have to be connected to your thoughts. If I am, I can pull you from the past and back into your future body."

"How would I know if your future self is linked to my mind?"

"He—me—I would try to communicate with your thoughts. You would be able to hear my voice in your head. But the only way to know for sure is having my grandfather place you in hypnosis again. If you hear my voice—the future me—in your head, then—"

"—I can go home."

"Yes. But no guarantees. Remember, our minds must be linked at the same time. Here and in the future."

"It's been several days now since I've been trapped in my teenage self," I said. "Do you really think your future self would bother to link minds again at this point—after so much time has passed?"

"I would be optimistic that I would," he replied with a reassuring smile. "I would not want you to die."

That was good enough for me. I gave him a nod, followed him into the foyer. As we reached the front door, and he opened it, I stopped in the doorway, and looked at him.

"By the way," I said. "I'm not married to a rich man just yet. How am I going to pay for this?"

"No charge," he replied.

I smiled, lifting my chin, moving my head to let him know how grateful I was to him. "Thank you."

"I'll be waiting for your call," he said. "Safe travels."

With that, he closed the door, and Steve and I walked to his car. Before we got in, I stopped to lean my head back and gaze toward the evening skyline.

"What's wrong?" Steve asked.

"I still can't believe this—that I'm here. Here, in the past. Reliving this. Breathing this. Going through this. I just want the nightmare to be over."

"I'm sure you do."

I lowered my head, looking in Steve's direction. "Even if Elroy Leonard dies, I still want to go back. I have to go back. I have to see my mother again—alive." I let out a sigh. "I just want to hear the sound of her voice again. Laugh with her again. And never have to worry about a future without her in it."

"Now you can have that," Steve said. "That super nerd's grandfather can make that happen. You can go back. Be with your mom. Prevent this from happening. Just promise me one thing…"

"What's that?"

"When you get back there, don't forget about me."

I smiled. "I won't."

I stayed alert the entire drive back home. I took the wheel from Steve halfway into the trip. He dozed off twice behind the wheel. He had been driving for several hours and needed to rest. As he slept across the back seat of his car, I deviated from our destination home. I decided to take a detour—straight to Elroy Leonard's house.

Steve had no idea I was going there, and when we arrived, I made sure not to wake him. I got out of the car, keeping the engine running, and the headlights on. I parked where we had parked the first time we were here. Where no one would see us. At least, I hoped.

At the time, I didn't know if Leonard was home or not. I found out later that he had been out at a bar binge drinking and getting into a fight with two patrons. He had beaten them bloody, and was arrested at the scene. As he sat in a jail, some miles away, I had made my way into his house, through the cellar, shooting off the padlock with two shots from my gun. The shots reverberated in the night air, but I didn't care. I'm sure I woke some of his neighbors, but it didn't matter to me anymore.

Vengeance mattered.

Getting to Leonard before he got to me or my family mattered.

Leonard had to die before I went back in time again. That was all that motivated me as I wandered around his basement cellar, my gun in one hand, a flashlight I got from Steve's car in the other. I knew what I was there for as I made my way through Leonard's makeshift meth lab.

I went for the paint thinner first, putting down my gun and the flashlight on a wooden workbench. I emptied the cannisters of paint thinner over the workbench, near the glass tubes, beakers, Bunsen burners, and large plastic containers where Leonard concocted his ingredients. I reached for the camping fuel and poured it along the cement floors, on the wooden stairs leading into the cellar, over piles of boxes, and emptied the rest over sheets hanging along a clothesline. Afterwards, I lit a match to the sheets, and watched in gratification as flames consumed them.

The fire filled the cellar in an instant and brought a feeling of redemption to my soul as my hand clenched into a fist at my side. I threw out my chest and sneered as if Elroy Leonard was the one burning in the flames. I watched the fire swirling in a dance toward the ceiling and found myself grinning at the destruction it caused.

I knew I wasn't just destroying the past. I was destroying the future. Leonard's future. And that made me feel good. It made me feel redeemed.

I became greedy for more, rushing over to the workbench, lighting the burners, and setting fire to the boxes and old wooden furniture Leonard had around the basement.

As the fire began to rage around me, I spat on the floor as I turned and made my way to the cellar entrance in a careless manner.

When I reached the backyard, I closed the cellar doors behind me and backed away from them as the inferno consumed the basement from my sight.

I walked around the house to the front yard and stood on the withered lawn, watching as the blaze rose from the cellar to the main floor, burning with a wrath and fury equal to what I felt in my heart.

I heard someone come running up behind me, and when I turned, I saw that it was Steve, his eyes wide and mouth dropped open.

"What happened?" he gawked.

I didn't respond. I returned my eyes to the burning house. I wanted to enjoy each moment of watching it consumed by the flames.

"Did you do this?" he asked.

I nodded my head with a slight grin of satisfaction.

Steve panicked. "What you do that for? That guy's really gonna be pissed now."

"I know," I said under my breath.

"Now you're an arsonist and a murderer! Are you ever going to go back to being that sweet girl from across the street?"

"Do you have paper and something to write with in the car?" I asked him, never removing my stare from the flames. The coldness of my tone made him edgy.

"Yeah, why?"

"Go get it. If you have scotch or duct tape, bring that too. I need to leave Leonard a little note."

"A note?"

"Yeah. I need to write: 'You know where to find me'. After that, I want you to tape the note to Leonard's fence. Where he can see it."

"Are you serious?" Steve asked. "You're really trying to draw him out?"

"You see his house on fire, don't you?"

Steve looked toward the house, shaking his head. He hesitated a moment before walking off, grumbling.

"Maybe Singh's grandfather can send me back in time instead."

I kept my focus on the house, watching as the flames consumed every layer of stone and wood, devouring everything in the home and sending thick black smoke and crackling sparks of fire spewing into the night air.

I stepped back and hunkered down to the ground, crossing my legs, sitting on the lawn, entranced by the flames. For the first time in my life since the murder of my mother, I felt as if I had control. Watching Elroy Leonard's home burn to ashes and explode from within... the destruction gave me a feeling of security I never had before.

For me.

For my brother.

For the future.

And I fell back onto the lawn, staring at the night sky, allowing myself to smile with a sense of victory.

CHAPTER TWENTY-SIX

THE POLICE RELEASED ELROY LEONARD from jail the following morning. The first thing he did, after stopping at a convenience store for aspirin and ginger ale, was drive straight home. When he saw the smoldering ruins still billowing black smoke into the morning air, he got out his pickup and ran toward what was left of his home.

The local fire department had arrived a few hours earlier, rummaging through the charred remains. The house had been burned to its foundation, and nothing remained of Elroy Leonard's material possessions within. He had thought the fire started from the meth lab he had in the cellar until the fire chief handed him the note I had left on his fence.

I later heard, that after crumbling the note in his hand, in an outburst of uncontrollable rage, he grabbed the fire chief by the jacket and roared:

"***That fucking bitch***!"

After that, he hopped into his vehicle and screeched off to find me.

The first place he went looking was our house. He kicked his way in through the back door, and stormed his way from the kitchen to the living room, but the house was empty by that time. My aunt and uncle had moved everything out. No memories that we had ever lived there was left behind. Nothing but an empty, lifeless structure with a "For Sale" sign staked into the lawn.

Enraged, Leonard left the house and got back into his pickup. He spent the next half hour driving around town searching for me until he realized what I meant in the note about knowing where to find me. That's when it hit him. He knew where I waited for him. The one place he had not revisited since removing the evidence he had left behind. The one place he knew harbored his evil deed.

And that's where I was. Waiting for him. Lighting candles in the same spot where he had taken my mother's life. Steve helped me light them. Forty-three in total. The age my mother was when she died.

When the last one was lit, I huddled it in the palm of my hands and set it in the middle of the parking space, centered to the other candles that encircled it.

I stepped back, away from the circle, and watched the flickering flames. Steve came over to my side, sighing.

"Why are you doing this?" he asked.

I didn't answer him.

"You don't have to do this now," he asserted. "You can go back to a time before any of this. You can change things—keep any of this from happening. Where's the sense in murdering this guy?"

"Satisfaction," I answered him. He sensed the pitiless tone in my voice.

"But it's wrong and you know it," he said. "We shouldn't even be here right now. We should be on our way back to the nerdy hypnotist's house."

I turned to Steve, balling my fist in rage. "And what if something else goes wrong? What if Singh's grandfather can't transport me back in time? What if my consciousness becomes lost somewhere in time? I'm not taking any chances. Elroy Leonard died in the first timeline. He can't survive! He's a threat! I can't let him live. The stakes are too high."

"So is the cost," Steve said. "For you."

I turned back toward the candles. "It's time for you to go now, Steve."

"What? What are you talking about?"

"I don't want you here when Leonard arrives. I want you far away from here. Go home. You'll be safe there."

"You really want me to leave you?"

"It's for your own safety."

"But what if you need my help. I mean, you'll be alone out here. This place is abandoned and far from any help if you need it. "

I took a deep breath. "I'll be fine, Steve. I don't want you to be a witness to this. It's going to get ugly. For either me or him."

He bit his lip, shook his head no. "I can't leave you. How are you supposed to get back to Singh's mansion?"

"Come back for me later."

"Anne…"

I turned and looked at him, ire in my eyes. "Go! Please. Just go. It'll be okay."

He turned, about to walk away, but stopped. "How do you know he's coming?"

"I sent him a clear message," I replied, looking over my shoulder before returning my gaze to the candles.

Steve sighed. "I wish I understood women better. I wish I understood bitter women even more."

He walked off, heading back toward his car. I watched him go, waiting until he was no longer in view.

The moment he disappeared through the adjacent, abandoned playground, a strange mist swooped in and skirted around the trees in the distance, rolling over the parking lot, erasing from view the asphalt that was there. It was the same fog I had seen in the dreams I had of my mother's death.

It came with a foreboding, swallowing the entire area—me with it. I had to squint my eyes to see two feet in front of me. An unnatural autumn breeze accompanied the strange mist, tousling my hair in its icy breath. I wrapped my arms around my upper body as my eyes struggled to pierce the fog.

I reached into the pocket of my blazer, clutching my gun. An eerie feeling came over me—one that felt all too familiar. A feeling I remembered from my dreams. The feeling that Elroy Leonard was near.

I started to pull the handgun from my blazer pocket when a gust of wind blew through me. A cold wind I had never felt before. Something sinister exemplified it.

I looked down toward the circle of candles and saw that the wind had blown out the flame to the center one. I removed my hand from my blazer pocket and placed it in the pocket of my jeans, where I had a lighter Steve had given to me on our way here.

I pulled the lighter from my pocket and knelt down before the candle. I hovered over it, blocking the wind as I lit it. When the flame rekindled its light, I smiled, feeling a calm happiness take over me. For a moment, I had become lost in the feeling, barricading my thoughts from where I was and why I was here. I wanted to relish the moment.

I inhaled the crisp air and the candlelight aroma around me, closing my eyes to take it all in. When I opened my eyes again, I looked around to make sure the other candles had not blown out. I placed the main candle back in the circle and stood to my feet. I took a moment to pull my emotions together. I felt a tug-of-war of sentiments wrestling within my soul. I knew I had to ignore them and regain concentration on the situation at hand.

In that moment, I looked away from the candles, about to turn—because some instinct inside me told me to—and I felt a presence, someone moving toward me. So I turned, and, just as I did, a powerful fist swung out of the thickening fog and struck my left cheekbone. The blow was fast and powerful, sending me reeling to the ground.

Before I had a chance to scream, a hulking figure was on top of me, grabbing me by the arm and blazer and yanking me from the ground, causing the handgun to fall from my blazer pocket.

"Crazy bitch! You burned down my house!"

It was Elroy Leonard, his voice inflamed with rage. His hands moved from my blazer to my throat, tightening, and not giving me any time to recover or regain my bearing or my breath. I was powerless, at his mercy, as he choked me.

He lifted my body inches from the ground and flung me through the air as if I weighed ten pounds.

The impact did more than knock the wind out of me. It caused me to see stars and black out for a moment. I tried to move, but screamed out in pain. The world around me was a blur.

Dazed, I tried to move my legs, but Leonard was on top of me again, grabbing me, and lifting me to my feet.

"You couldn't leave well enough alone," he rasped. "You had to keep fucking with me. I told you, I didn't have anything to do with what happened to your mother. That should have been good enough for you."

I spit blood in his face. "You're a liar."

He released me, and I collapsed to the ground.

He backed away from me, and wiped the blood with the sleeve of his denim jacket.

"I know what you did," I said, trying to crawl away from him. "You know what you did."

He looked down at me, his eyes narrowing in an ice-cold stare. "If I wanted to hurt you or your family I would have done so already. I was going to leave you alone. But you just had to go and push me."

"You started this," I sneered. "Look around—where we are. Remember this place? This is where you started this. This is where you took my mother's life. Right over there." I pointed toward the candles. "In that parking space. It's the last place my mother saw life."

He snarled and frowned instead of looking in the direction I was pointing. He kept his eyes on me. "You're out of your fucking mind."

"I saw her that night, in her car," I said, crawling away from him, my lip bleeding. "She met with you because she didn't think in a million years that you would kill her over a breakup. She trusted you.

She still cared for you. But you couldn't deal with being rejected. You couldn't let go. You wouldn't let her move on."

My words struck a nerve. His posture stooped and his mouth fell open, but no words were able to come out. He stood there, gawking at me, wondering how I knew the details of his crime that night without being there to witness it. That put fear in him. He was in a stupor, his eyes lowering, searching, trying to comprehend and figure out where he went wrong.

When he snapped out of it, he returned his attention back to me. "You don't know what you're talking about."

He knew that I did, but he wouldn't admit it. He was never going to confess to the crime. Not while he was still a free man. And not without the evidence the police needed to convict him.

I got to my feet, wiping the blood from my lip. "Don't I?" I stared at him, boring my eyes into his. "You waited for her. Right over there in the abandoned playground. Drinking yourself into a frenzy. You left behind those beer cans."

"I told you before. I was never here that night."

"When she arrived," I went on, "you pulled the hood over your head, made sure no one was around, then you got into her car. You tried to plead with her to take you back, but she didn't. That's when you got angry and hit her. She hit you back. You started fighting. She tried to get away from you, but you pulled out that knife and stabbed her with it. Over and over again. Until she stopped moving. Until she stopped breathing."

I had him where I wanted him. Distracted. Dumfounded. Shaking his head in disbelief. I had him sweating.

"You almost got away with it," I said. "But the police found the beer cans and your fingerprints on them. Then they found the knife you used. Where you always kept it. Where it is right now. In your back pocket."

He lowered his head, halfway looking back, toward his back pocket. He looked back at me. *How did I know that?*

"You'll never admit what you did," I said, wiping blood from my lip. "I see that now. You're a coward. You don't have any regrets because you don't have a fucking conscious."

He snarled again. I had his number and called him out for who and what he was, and he didn't like it.

"You didn't get away with it then,' I asserted. "And you won't get away with it now."

I looked past him, toward the parking space, where my handgun had fallen. I saw it, next to the center candle. I knew I had to distract him and get to it.

He looked at me, unable to respond, the shock and disbelief widening his eyes as his brain searched for answers. His mind wondering how I knew what I knew.

That's when I went for it. I took off running toward the parking space, darting past him. But the pain from my elbow and the injury to my wrist set in and diminished my chances of out running him. He managed to catch me with a single lunge, grasping the back of my blazer and yanking me back.

I reacted fast, slipping my arms out of the sleeves of the blazer. At that moment, I remembered my future training in self defense, and went for his crotch with a swift kick. But my attack missed his privates and struck his thigh instead. I had to counter with a straight jab to his face, striking him in the cheek.

The blow didn't faze him.

It was as if a rubber mallet struck a petrified tree stump.

I tried again, this time with the injured wrist I sustained after Leonard ran me off the road. But he deflected that blow with his shoulder, and shoved me to the ground. He stood over me, holding me down with one arm while reaching for the knife in his back pocket with the other.

I tried to kick and punch my way to freedom, but my teenage body was too fragile, and at the mercy of his powerful grasp. He had his weight on me, pinning my legs. I fought him with my free arm. But my slaps and punches hurt me more than him.

"No one's ever gonna know what happened here," he growled.

Then he grimaced as he pulled the knife from his back pocket and brandished it over me, my mother's blood dried on the handle and blade. He held it up over his head and drove it down into my thigh.

I let out a gurgling screech that penetrated the morning silence. I tried reaching for the wound, but Leonard sank the blade deeper into it, twisting the blade in his hand. He growled as he removed it from the wound and lifted it into the air again.

This time he drove the blade into my shoulder, tearing flesh into shreds as he rotated the weapon in his grasp. I didn't let out a scream. Instead, I became determined to keep him from killing me. I scratched his face with my nails, tearing away flesh. I shifted my head and gnawed into his hand. He let out a grunt, but he didn't release his hold on the knife. I tried to get my claws into his face again, but he yanked the blade from my shoulder and drove it back into the wound.

I cried out in agony, my eyes tearing from the pain.

He had me where he wanted me, and he took pleasure in that truth. I didn't have the strength to defend myself. My teenage body weakened and I felt my muscles and nerves go lifeless. My eyelids became a burden to keep open. I relented and watched as Leonard raised the knife again, priming himself for one final blow to my heart.

I turned my head away and closed my eyes.

Then—

The shot rang out like a clap of thunder from the heavens, echoing throughout the parking lot.

I heard the bullet rip through Elroy Leonard's upper body, piercing flesh and blood.

He made no sound.

I opened my eyes and looked up at him. His expression had shifted from rage to shock. His eyes widened and became bloodshot red. The knife dropped from his grip and fell to the ground next to me. Then, with a grunt, his bulky body capsized over me.

Despite my injuries, I elevated my head to see where the gunshot had come from.

Through the fog, I saw Steve standing in the parking space near the lit candles, holding my handgun.

I took a moment to catch my breath, struggling to get to my feet. I had to drag myself toward Steve. The knife wound to my leg sent sharp pangs through every vein.

I kept my eyes on Leonard the entire time, watching him roll over and use his arms to stand. But he fell to his knees, coughing.

When I reached Steve, he was trembling beyond control.

"I never shot anyone before," he said. "He was going to kill you. I wouldn't have done it if he wasn't going to kill you. I had no choice, Anne."

I looked at him, allowing myself a weak smile. I hugged him tight.

"It's okay," I said, my voice weak. "I know."

"He was going to kill you," he repeated. "I saw him stab you. I heard you screaming. You were going to die. I wouldn't have shot him if you weren't going to die."

"It's okay, Steve," I said, moving back and away from him as I reached my hand out for the gun. "You did well. Give me the gun. It's okay."

He hesitated, still trembling.

"Everything's okay," I promised him. "Give me the gun."

He handed me the gun, almost dropping it. He let out a breath and grabbed his knees.

"You're okay, Steve," I said, soft enough to relax him. "Everything's going to be okay."

"Oh, man, I hope so," he said in a shaky voice. "I don't want to go to prison. I'm not built for jail."

"You're not going to jail," I said. "Everything is going to be fine."

He nodded his head with several nervous movements as he tried to catch his breath and keep himself from hyperventilating. "Okay, okay."

"Go get the car."

He hurried off in a panic.

I waited until he was gone before limping toward Elroy Leonard. The world slowed to a crawl and the wind diminished to an eerie whisper. I no longer heard the morning singing of the birds. The fog began to dissipate as I moved through it, swirling aside to allow me passage.

Elroy Leonard did not hear me approaching. He had his hand pressured against the wound the bullet left in his upper shoulder. He rocked back and forth for a moment, until he realized I was standing over him. He turned his head, looked up at me. I saw the rage in his narrowing eyes. Then he looked away as I raised the gun, steadying it in my hand.

"Go ahead," he said. "Do what you gotta do, bitch."

"With pleasure," I spat back. Then I pulled the trigger.

The bullet exploded from the muzzle in sparks and smoke. The recoil jerked my arm back as the round tore through the air on target, lodging its way into the side of Elroy Leonard's head.

I watched as his body fell to the ground, convulsing for a moment, before going limp. I hobbled back toward the candles, satisfied, for the moment.

But something told me to stop, to look back, to make sure he was dead.

I turned and looked back at him. He wasn't breathing. But I had to make sure.

I staggered back to the body, peering down at his corpse, waiting for him to move, keeping the gun on him.

He didn't move. His eyes were rolled up in his head and he bled from his mouth and nose. Nevertheless, I shot him again in the head.

No movement.

He was down for good.

I exhaled a long breath, relieved, dropping to one knee while releasing my hold on the gun and allowing it to drop by my side. I began to cry.

It was over.

Over at last.

Elroy Leonard was dead…

Again.

CHAPTER TWENTY-SEVEN

I WAS IN AND OUT OF CONSCIOUSNESS during the drive back to the younger Professor Singh's mansion. Steve had shredded my blazer and used the torn rags to staunch the knife wounds. It stopped the bleeding—somewhat—but not the pain.

The throbbing in my shoulder made me sick, almost as if I had to vomit. The pain came in intense ripples, sometimes in sharp pangs, sometimes in deaden hammerings, around the inside of the wound. The gash in my leg still felt as if someone was punching me in the laceration. It didn't sting as bad as the knife wound in my shoulder, but it bothered me way more than the leg wound.

Lucky for me, the blade missed the femoral artery, and Steve was able to clot the wound and bandage it to keep it from getting infected. He had his hand over the wound while driving.

"I think the bleeding stopped," he said. "Still gotta get you to the hospital."

"There's no time for that," I responded. "Just keep driving."

"You got stabbed," he expressed with anxiety in his tone. "Those wounds need to be treated by a doctor. You definitely need stitches."

"If you get me to Singh's, I don't have to worry about these wounds," I pointed out, struggling to smile without revealing the pain I was in.

Steve kept shaking his head.

"Steve," I said. "If I go to the hospital, they're going to want to know what happened. Just keep driving and everything will be all right."

Steve looked at me, a nervous wreck. After a moment, he agreed with me, nodding his head. He drove for several moments in silence. But I saw that something else was bothering him. He kept biting his lip and breathed in quick breaths. His hands shook at the steering wheel and he seemed distracted as he drove.

"Something else is bothering you," I said. "What is it?"

He glanced at me, his mouth open, but no words came out.

"Spit it out," I pressed him. "Say what you feel."

He let out a long breath. "I still can't believe that guy's dead. And we—we killed him."

"You didn't kill him, Steve. I did."

"I shot him, though."

"To save me." I forced my body into an upright position, moaning from the pain in my shoulder and leg. "Listen, Steve, you didn't do anything wrong. There's no blood on your hands. The blood is on my hands. I'm the one who came back in time and took the lives of three people. I'm the one who has to live with that. The only thing you should be living with right now is that you saved my life."

"Yeah, well, you still need a doctor for those wounds," he grumbled.

I smiled, sinking into the seat and closing my eyes to rest.

Before I knew it, I was dreaming. Or I thought it was a dream. I didn't see any clouded images in my mind. Instead, I heard a familiar voice. It was the voice of Professor Singh—the future Professor Singh.

He must have connected with my mind in the future again. The young Singh said he would, which meant that my future body was still alive. His voice was faint, distant, but it was him, calling my name out in echoes, reaching into my consciousness.

I knew the best thing for me to do at that point was allow myself, my consciousness, to let go and drift away. Not to fight against him as I did before. I fell into a trance, and I felt my essence, my mind, pulling away from my teenage self.

Somewhere between the consciousness of my teenage self and my body in the future, I felt my eyes blinking. But I wasn't able to open them.

I heard Professor Singh's voice getting closer and closer, as if he was walking toward me, but I did not answer him. I felt the pressure of his fingers against the temples of my head. He was trying to bring me back.

"Anne, wake up," he commanded. "Open your eyes."

But I heard another voice calling out to me at the same time. It was Steve, shouting, his voice shaky, frightened.

"Anne! **Anne! Wake up!**"

I felt someone shaking me, but I wasn't sure who. I drifted in and out of consciousness from my teenage body to my future self, my eyes blinking in both the past and the future worlds. Both Professor Singh's voice and Steve's resonated in my head again and again, pulling my consciousness into a back and forth rivalry.

"Anne, if I lose you again, this is it. I can't keep you alive in this time. Your body dies here. I won't be able to reach your consciousness again."

His voice drifted in and out. When it came back, he said, "Only you can release yourself from the past. Only you can let go. If you don't, your consciousness and soul will remain in the past. You must snap out of it. You must come back into your present body. Wake up. Wake up."

I heard another voice. It was Steve. He was in my head, too, shouting over and over again, "You need to get up now! Come on! Wake up!"

I felt the lids of my eyes moving irregularly as they began to open, sluggish and blurred.

I didn't have a sense of where I was, at first—the present or the past. The voices in my head had silenced and the world around me hushed itself.

Where was I? I wondered. *Did I make it back into my future body? Was the nightmare finally over?*

I opened my eyes all the way and realized I was still in Steve's car.

I sat up in the seat, looking around, my vision clouded, trying to regain a sense of where I was.

"What—what's happening?"

In a trembling voice, Steve responded, "The police are on my tail."

I looked in the rearview-mirror, turning around to see a police cruiser following us.

"He's been behind us for like two blocks," Steve said. "I thought you had died on me or something. Where the hell did you go?"

"Somewhere I can never get back to now," I answered him.

"What should I do?" Steve asked. He was way past playing it cool. He struggled to keep a firm grasp on the steering wheel.

"How far are we from Singh's?" I asked him.

"We got several more blocks," he wailed. "I don't think we're going to make it."

"Relax, Steve, he hasn't pulled us over yet."

"Yeah, but, he's tailing us. That's a very, very bad sign."

"Just drive calmly. Be nonchalant. Don't keep looking in the mirror."

"I can't help it. I can't stop shaking. He's gotta be following us for a reason."

I agreed with Steve in silence, widening my eyes to keep them focused and alert on what the officer inside the car was doing. I turned around in my seat, straightened my posture, and locked my eyes to the side-view mirror.

The police cruiser kept its distance, but I saw the cop inside talking on the radio. He must've been talking to the dispatch at his police station. I looked at Steve.

"I think he's running your plate," I said to him.

"What?"

"He's probably checking because of where we are," I said, trying to make Steve feel better. "This is an upscale neighborhood and we have out of town plates."

"You think so?" Steve had a moment of relief.

"It has to be. That's why he hasn't pulled us over."

"I hope so. I've seen enough police since you knocked at my door. I don't ever want to see another cop again."

"Just try and relax."

I kept my eyes on the mirror, watching the police cruiser's every move.

"Turn at this next corner, Steve. I want to see something."

Steve turned, and so did the cop.

"Uh-oh."

"What?" Steve was about to panic again.

"He's definitely after us. If he pulls us over, he's going to ask questions. And we don't have any time for questions."

"Or jail," Steve said.

That hopeful moment of relief left him as fast as it came. He started biting at a fingernail and babbling to himself.

"I knew I shouldn't have opened that door. I knew I should have went to college after graduating. How did I get myself into this?"

I checked the side-view mirror again. The police cruiser sped up, flashing its sirens.

"Shit!" I cried out.

Steve looked in the rearview-mirror and eyed the cruiser closing in.

"Oh, no, no, no!" He freaked out. "What do I do now?"

"Stay calm," I told him. "Pull over."

Steve pulled over to the curb, in front of a luxurious home.

"Should I get out of the car?" Steve asked.

"No," I answered. "But whatever you do, don't turn off the engine."

He nodded and placed his hands on his lap, fidgeting, his eyes moving from his side-view mirror to the mounted mirror on the windshield. He kept fidgeting until I grabbed his arm.

"Relax," I said.

I looked back and watched as the officer got out of the cruiser and started walking toward our car. When he reached the driver's side, he looked in the car—maybe checking for weapons or drugs—or maybe following routine procedure. He removed his sunglasses and looked from Steve to me.

Right away, he seemed suspicious, but he didn't show it in his posture or mannerisms. He showed it the moment he placed his hand on his holstered revolver.

"Morning, officer," Steve said. "Did I do something wrong?"

"Is this your car?" he asked.

"Yes, sir, it is," Steve answered. "Did I do something wrong?"

"You have your vehicle registration and driver's license with you?" The cop followed protocol, remaining resigned, yet sharp-eyed.

"Sure do." Steve reached into his pocket, pulling out his wallet and handing the cop his driver's license and registration.

The officer scrutinized Steve's I.D. Afterwards, something made him look in my direction. He noticed the bloodstained bandages on my leg and shoulder.

"What happened to you?" he asked.

I put on my happy face, smiling.

"I was out hiking this morning and fell into a trench," I responded, laughing to myself. "Being careless. I injured my shoulder and leg in the fall. Fell into a bunch of sharp twigs and thorns."

"You're still bleeding," he observed. "Maybe you need medical attention."

"I plan on going to the doctor when I get back home," I said. "We're on our way to my cousin's house. He has a first aid kit in his house. I figured he can patch me up until I get home to see my doctor."

"Where does your cousin live?" he asked.

"Just around the corner from here," I answered.

He looked at Steve, who gazed straight ahead, avoiding eye contact. The cop knew something was wrong, but he didn't let us know what that something was. He played it cool. Nothing out of the ordinary for a police officer.

"I need to run your license and check your registration. Sit tight. I'll be back."

"Okay, officer, thank you," Steve said, forcing a smile. But it was not convincing.

The police officer walked away, heading back to his cruiser. I reached out and clutched Steve's wrist.

"I told you to stay calm."

"I tried," he responded. "I really did."

I looked in the mirror and watched the officer as he climbed into his cruiser, biting my lip and slumping in my seat as an uneasy feeling came over me.

"He pulled us over for a reason," I said to Steve. "Only he knows what that reason is."

"You think it has something to do with that Leonard guy?" Steve wondered.

"It just might," I responded.

"Damn it!" Steve cried out. "And we just left his body lying there out in the opening of that parking lot for anyone to come across."

"Him… and the gun that killed him."

Steve looked at me through bulging eyes and quick breaths. "Oh, no. I forgot about that. What we do now? What do we do?"

My skin felt clammy. I knew I had to think fast and make a move. I thought about the future—the one that I would have if I made it back to an earlier time than the one I was in now.

I grabbed Steve's hand and looked back at the cruiser, making sure I still had time before the police officer made his way back to our car.

"You have to let me out," I said to Steve. "I have to make a run for it. I can't afford to stop now."

"How far do you think you'll get on foot with your injuries? You'll never make it. That cop will catch you."

"Maybe you can distract him."

"For how long? He'll notice you gone and go after you."

"Steve, if the police found Leonard's body…"

"I know, I know. But you gotta come up with a better plan than making a run for it."

"I'm trying to come up with the plan that doesn't involve you going to jail over my mistakes."

"Too late for that one. Try another."

"You're being difficult."

"Maybe because my heart is racing here."

I looked back over the seat, out the back window, and saw the police officer get out of his cruiser and walk back toward the car.

"Shit. Here he comes."

Steve's eyes darted from the side-view mirror to the rearview-mirror, and back to me. The look in his eyes told me he was about to do something drastic. But before I was able to utter a word, he put the car in drive and hit the gas pedal.

"What are you doing?" I shouted in a shaken voice.

"We're only a few blocks away," Steve responded. "We can still make it."

"I don't want you doing this," I pleaded. "Stop the car, Steve!"

Instead of stopping, he slammed his foot down on the gas pedal harder than before, and the car roared up the street, taking corners at dangerous speeds. I reached for the seatbelt, but the car was taking turns too fast for me to fasten it.

I heard the police siren whir behind us, but the police cruiser did not appear in the rearview-mirror. We had the jump on it, and managed to stay a block ahead of it. Steve had the faster car. But what he didn't have was back up. The cop did. And the sound of more sirens responding to the pursuit echoed around us. They were closing in.

That was fast, I thought to myself. Either they had more cruisers in the immediate vicinity or he had called them ahead of our getaway. I considered the latter. *How else did they respond that fast?* That meant they knew about the murder.

The police in our county must've found Elroy Leonard's body and sent out an all-points bulletin to law enforcement agencies in other counties.

I didn't contemplate the police finding Leonard's body that fast in an abandoned parking lot. But I later discovered that someone walked their dog in that parking lot every morning and came across the corpse.

Once again, I had been careless.

And this time, it was going to cost me my future.

I wanted Steve to stop the car and make his own getaway— without having to worry about me. However, I knew he wouldn't. The wetness in his eyes, his heavy panting, signaled the desperation that now ran through his mind. He was no longer afraid. He was determined.

When we screeched around another corner, he raced toward the driveway of a deluxe home and backed the car into the driveway. Sweating, he looked at me and shouted, "Get out!"

"What?"

"Singh's house is the next block over," he said. "You can make it from here. Cut through the yard. I'll keep the cops busy. Let them chase me around. That should give you some time."

"Steve—"

"—There's no time," he interrupted. "Go now."

I hesitated, and he reached over and opened the passenger side door, pushing me out.

"Go!" he shouted. "Go! You can make it!"

I hurried from the vehicle and ran toward the backyard of the house. I stopped and turned back as Steve shut the door and drove off, the rubber of his tires burning tread marks into the pavement.

I hid behind a garbage can and watched as Steve's car disappeared around a corner. A moment later, the police cruiser appeared, fast-tracking past the house in hot pursuit. The cop inside the car didn't see me. The moment he turned the corner, hot on Steve's trail, I made a run for it, racing through the backyard, hopping over fences, with my injured leg and shoulder hampering my agility and speed.

My heart raced faster than my body.

Every scrambling motion I had to make hurt like hell. And I felt the blood spurting from my wounds. But I had to keep moving. I rallied the will and tenacity to oppose my pain and shuffle my way from one backyard through the next until I came out onto a main street again.

I took cover behind a tree as another police cruiser blared past me. I waited until it reached the end of the neighborhood street before hobbling my way through the backyard of another house.

My breaths were getting shorter, and my shoulder felt as if someone had branded it with a hot iron. I took a moment to rest and catch my breath near a garden. I listened for the police sirens, but did not hear them anymore. Steve must have led them away from the surrounding neighborhoods.

I took a few deep breaths and started moving again. I made my way from the backyard and into the street. Singh's house stood a long dash away. But I convinced myself that I would make it if I ran for it now. If I hesitated, my injuries would ebb what little strength I had left.

The young Singh appeared in his doorway as I began rushing toward the house. A taxi cab had pulled into the courtyard, and an old man dressed in a bright yellow Kurta and turban got out.

Singh's grandfather.

It had to be him.

They both greeted each other with slight bows, their hands placed together, a customary respect I've seen before in my travels abroad with my husband—my future husband. I grinned to myself the moment I saw them. They were a few yards away—within running distance—which meant I was almost there, nearer to safety and that much closer to being transported once again into the past to undo the mess I made in this timeline.

The feeling of attainment rushed over me and prompted my legs to hasten. I counted every pace forward, pushing myself harder.

I was almost there. Almost.

Another fifty feet… I would have made it. But, out of nowhere, police cruisers appeared from both directions on the street, blocking my path to the house.

I locked my gaze on the young Singh and his grandfather, ignoring everything else around me. I had one objective: *get to the house*. I never played sports in my life, but, at that moment, I imagined myself as an athlete, a running back, holding the football, and rushing for the touchdown.

I headed for the police as they sprang from their vehicles, guns drawn. They moved in to make the arrest, tackling me from both sides. It took four of them to apprehend me and bring me to the ground. I kicked and screamed, mobilizing the strength to fight them, but it was to no avail. I felt the cold metal of handcuffs hook around my wrists.

"Stop resisting," one of the officers said. "You're only going to hurt yourself."

"You don't understand!" I cried out. "You have to let me go! I need to get to that house! They're waiting for me right there! They're right there! You have to let me go!"

"Just take it easy," the officer responded, as the other three officers lifted me to my feet.

"Please," I begged through teary eyes. "They're right there. I can still make it. My future depends on it."

But they ignored me as they searched me, patting me down, no words exchanged between them.

I had no strength left to wrestle against them. I relinquished my strength to their custody, catching my breath. My shoulder and leg wounds saturated the torn cloth from my blazer with more blood from my stab wounds. I had cuts and bruises all over my face and upper body. My posture deflated and drooped as I realized I had lost.

I stood there a moment, eyeing the young Singh and his grandfather as they walked from the courtyard to the sidewalk to see what was going on. When the young Singh recognized who I was, his mouth dropped open from the shock. He walked to the end of the driveway, watching helplessly.

I wanted to call out to him, but failure and humiliation muffled my voice. Instead, I turned away, lowering my head. I was now destined to live out the rest of my days in the past, and I had no one to blame.

I sealed my own fate. But, as long as Elroy Leonard was dead, I was okay with that.

CHAPTER TWENTY-EIGHT

Dear Andy:

I hope this letter reaches you and finds you sound and better off than the time I left you in before.

I know you will not understand my actions or what I've done. I can never explain them so that you would understand why I did what I did. Or why I left you. I know that's going to be the hardest part of this to deal with. Me not being there when you need me the most. But I am there. I've always been. Always will be. I know that sounds hard to understand or to believe, but I am there with you. I have never abandoned you. You kept me alive. You gave me a purpose. Both in the future and in the past.

I know this will sound confusing to you, and you're probably asking yourself, what the hell is she talking about? But I can't explain it to you. I can never explain it to you. Your not knowing keeps you safe. It changes your future as it has done mine. Yours for the better. Mine for the worse. But I did what I had to do. I would've wanted to change it where we would have all been together again—you, me and mother—happy again as a family. But fate saw otherwise. Or my actions did.

Remember what I told you when I came to see you that night.

Always remember my words. Because they're more than words. They're instructions.

You must never let our mother's death change you in a bad way. You must never become consumed by rage and vengeance and hatred. Like I did. Those emotions will destroy you. And you must never let my actions give you mixed emotions about people. Some are good, others are lost. But no one deserves to die. Not by our hands. No matter what they did to us. I only did what I did to save you. That doesn't make what I did right. But it was necessary.

Our wounds can never heal over time, but they can mend. I know yours will. I know you will never forget, but never let the bitterness and hurt consume you. Promise me that you will live your life to the fullest. It is all I ever wanted for you. To see you whole. Strong. Promise me you will never waste a day of your life. That good will come from the pain of what was taken from us. Do good. There are people out there who are going to need you. They are either going through or have experienced the same thing as you and I have. They will need therapy and counselling. They will need support. When you get old enough, help them. Help them by being there for them.

We can never change the world we live in, Andy, but we cannot allow the dark things in it to change us. Remember that, Andy. Always remember what our family life was like before Elroy Leonard took it away from us. Always remember that we were fortunate to have the mother we did… even if it was for a little while. That is what is worth cherishing. That… and the meaning your life has to me. Never forget that. And never forget:

"Choices create circumstances; decisions determine your future" That's taken from John Croyle. Remember those words.

I will always love you, Andy.

Your sister,

Anne

CHAPTER TWENTY-NINE

"WAKE UP, DONOVAN, your lawyer's here to see you."

The sound of the prison guard's orotund voice woke me out of a deep sleep as he entered my minimum security dormitory. I sat up in my single-cell bunk stretching my arms and yawning. I lifted my head and snapped my neck, removing a crick.

"Yeah, okay," I responded.

I put on the shoes under my bunk and got to my feet with my eyes half open. I didn't comb my hair or brush my teeth. I didn't care. I didn't care about my appearance or the pungency of my breath. I moved with nothing to live for.

I had learned to live with my fate behind bars. Even though I hadn't come to terms with age yet. I was now the exact age I had been when my consciousness and essence were sent back in time through hypnosis.

I hadn't aged into that wealthy woman who afforded the best skin-care treatments and manicures.

The mirror on the wall of my cell reflected my reality the moment I crossed paths with it as I walked toward the guard standing at the solid steel doors. I stopped to look at myself, reminded of what time behind bars and apathy did to a person.

My body had aged to sagging breasts and lined skin texture. My once lustrous hair had strands of gray that limply outlined my cranky expression. I no longer had the sophistication and softness I had in the original timeline of my existence. My forehead wrinkled into crests and furrows from a life of fixed frowning.

I held my hands up to my face and examined how weathered and coarse they had become. All of this time had passed, and I never realized how unkind I had been to myself.

"Donovan," the guard called from the door. "Your lawyer's waiting. Let's go."

I dropped my hands to my sides, looked at my lined face one last time in the mirror, and made my way to the door.

The guard escorted me from my cell to an open area where the guards had maximum visibility of the inmates and their guests. Rows of metal tables and chairs filled the area. Several inmates walked around chatting with each other, while others read books, played on their iPads, or met with visitors.

I saw the man who had come to see me. He sat at one of the metal tables, closer to the sitting room window looking out to the prison courtyard where we stretched our legs and exercised for two hours a day. A woman, who I didn't know, sat next to him, dressed in an expensive business suit. She looked rich.

As I made my way to the table, I fixed my gaze on him, staring at him with my chin held high, pride in my stride and expression.

He sat at the table, with his fine gray suit, tailored to his wiry frame, and his blue eyes peering through expensive black-rimmed Cartier eyeglasses framed to his face. He ran his hand through his warm brown hair as he went through his paperwork. The woman next to him moved closer to touch him, her eyes making a strong connection to his eyes.. I realized she was attracted to him.

Who wouldn't be?

He was handsome from the color of his eyes to the fine and seamlessly symmetrical bone structure of his face. When I had seen that face before—before the hypnotic time travel—it had been twisted by despair and misery and neglect and malnourishment. Now it was a full, chiseled face, beaming from a life of prosperity and health.

I sat across from him and the woman, and he smiled the moment he saw me, looking up from the paperwork he had spread out in front of him. I looked from him to the woman, and back to him, unable to screen my happiness as I folded my arms and crossed my legs, trying to appear stern.

"Well, well. It's been nearly six months," I said. "I thought you forgot about me."

"You know I could never do that," he smiled back. "I've been busy working on getting you out of here. And other things."

He looked at the woman. They both smiled at each other. It was lovey-dovey emotions for sure. He looked away from her, returning his stare to me.

"How've you been, sis?"

"Missing your visits, Andy," I answered.

"I know," he said. "Don't think you haven't been on my mind."

I looked at the woman sitting next to him. "On your mind, but apparently distracted."

"A good distraction," he said, looking at the woman, taking her hand into his own. "Anne, this is Kate Donovan."

I looked at them agape. "Donovan?"

"We married three weeks ago," he said. "I originally met her last year when she came to work for our firm. I never mentioned her before because—well, you know—with your case and all. It never seemed right to talk about anything else outside of getting you out of prison."

"I understand."

"We fell in love—mainly working late hours on your case—and we decided to get married. I wanted to surprise you. I would have done so sooner, but so many things got in the way. I wanted to wait until we got you out of prison, but--"

"I told you I understand."

Kate took her eyes away from my brother to address me. "It's a pleasure to finally meet you, Anne."

She seemed cordial and attentive, more than a blonde beauty, but a woman having an excess of energy and enthusiasm with a level head. I couldn't have been happier for the both of them, and they knew that the moment they noticed my smile.

"I hope you're not angry with us for getting married without you there?" Kate said. "And then not telling you."

I kept my arms folded and legs crossed, maintaining my rigid posture. It took a moment, but my response came with a cracking voice. "I wish I would have been there to see my baby brother get married. But knowing that he's happy, that's all that matters to me."

Andy smiled, glancing at his paperwork. "Well, like I said, we've been working day and night on getting you pardoned. It's been tough. You know that. Especially after your initial trial. They had the murder weapon with your fingerprints on it. They had a motive. Revenge— though they could never prove Elroy Leonard actually murdered our mother—even after finding the knife he used at the crime scene. The prints were all him, but a prosecution argued that you planted the knife on him to make him look guilty. I don't know how they were able to convince a jury of that. Basically, the state had a strong prosecutor and you had a weak defense."

I looked around the prison. "That's obvious."

Andy straightened his posture. "I'm sorry, sis."

"I took a life… they gave me life."

"Your life's not going to end behind prison walls," Andy said. "I was never going to let that happen."

I looked toward the window, pensive. "Maybe it's time you do, Andy. It's been over three decades. I'm used to this life. I'm used to not looking forward to anything else but your happiness. It's the only thing that made the sacrifice worthwhile."

"And fighting for your freedom has made my life worth it," Andy retorted.

"I've been moved around to three different prisons in the last thirty something years. I've watched myself age into a woman I barely recognize. But I will never lose any sleep over my actions. I admitted murdering that son of a bitch. I enjoyed watching him die. And I would relive that moment every single day if I could. There are no regrets. Just for his brother and the woman with him and not being able to save our mom. Outside of that, I can live with my choices. I don't want you to have any regrets, neither. So, please, enjoy your life. I'm still here if and when you need me. But I want you to move on."

Andy's eyes watered. "You once told me to promise you that I would do everything in my power to reach my goals. Remember that? This is my goal, Anne. Getting you out of here. I haven't rested in that goal. That's why we're here today." He looked at his wife. "Tell her."

"Anne, we've gone through your case a million times since Andy asked me to review it. What happened, at the time, was that the prosecution was able to prove beyond a reasonable doubt that you committed first degree murder."

"I did."

"Yes, I know that."

"The death of Elroy Leonard was deliberate and premeditated. The prosecution proved that because it was a fact. I never denied that. I confessed to that."

"They found the murder weapon you used," Kate said, looking through a file. "They obtained evidence and witnesses that you purchased the illegal firearm and planned to use it in the death of Elroy Leonard."

"That's already been established," I said. *Where was she going with this?* "There's no reason to relive my motives."

"I know," Kate responded. "This is what went wrong with your case. The defense couldn't argue the facts or the evidence. You confessed to the crime, but during your trial, no witnesses were brought forth on your behalf, even after the police interrogated one Steve Mitchell about his relationship with you. He said in a sworn statement that you told him you had traveled from the future and into the past to prevent the death of your mother at the hands of Elroy Leonard."

She looked at me as if she was expecting me to deny what I had confessed to Steve. She didn't believe it herself. She stared into me, looking to see if any evidence was there of me being crazy. When I remained unresponsive, she looked through my file again.

"I looked at other statements we came across," she went on. "You had also told the police, that after your mother was murdered, you believed Leonard was the man who committed the crime. The police questioned Leonard at the time, but had no evidence to hold him on. Not until they found the knife he used at the crime scene where you shot him. He used that knife on you. A year later, one Detective Kelly looked into the case again, and, through DNA evidence, found that the weapon Leonard used on you was also used on your mother. The police found your mother's DNA on the knife when the technology allowed them to. This proved that Leonard had indeed used it on your mother that terrible night. You were the only one who knew at the time Leonard had committed that crime."

"I'm no lawyer, but it sounds to me like you're saying I could've pleaded self-defense," I said.

"No," Andy answered. "Not self-defense. You left a note for Leonard. Your handwriting was on it. You led him to the parking lot where you shot him. If anything, he could have pleaded self-defense for stabbing you."

"Okay, I'm confused, then," I said, looking at the both of them. "If my defense couldn't argue self-defense, what then?"

"Insanity," Andy said. "Sworn statements from people you told you were from the future, existing in your teenage body. Whether people believed it or not, you believed it. That convinced the three psychologists who examined you after your conviction that mom's murder left you mentally and emotionally unstable. A sane person just doesn't go around telling people they're future self is inhabiting their present teenage body. Medical professionals made written diagnosis that you were, at the time, suffering from mental illness that caused your inability to control your actions or conform yourself to conduct to the law."

"It would have been a weak defense," I told Andy. "My crime was premeditated. The state proved that. I never showed any signs of being insane. I still don't. Depending on who you ask around here."

"Anne—" Andy started to say, but I interrupted him.

"Andy, two attorneys filed appeals on my behalf before you completed college. Both attempts were unsuccessful."

"Those appeals weren't to Supreme Courts," Andy retorted.

"It doesn't matter now. It's too late. The attorneys failed to get critical, available evidence into the record. The opportunity to do so now is lost. Double jeopardy. No retrials. I just have to live with the sentence."

"Not anymore," Andy said with a slight smile.

"What do you mean?"

"That's what I came here to tell you, Anne." He looked at his wife, smiling. "We got the governor to give you a full pardon."

I uncrossed my legs and leaned forward, eyeing both of them. I unfolded my arms and clutched the ends of the table. It was the only way I could stop my body from trembling as an adrenaline rush came over me.

"Are you serious?"

Kate smiled. "Given the circumstances of your case and new evidence, the governor agreed to unconditionally absolve you of the conviction and all of the crime's consequences."

Andy reached over the table and took my hands into his own. "I never stopped fighting for you, sis. I know you would've done the same for me. Now, I can finally take you back home… where you belong."

I fought back tears. "I can't believe this."

Andy leaned back, looking at his wife, smiling, kissing her on the cheek. He looked at me, his eyes watering. "We're family. That was always important to mom. And I know it was important to you. We're all that we have. If it wasn't for you, I would've never pursued law. I would've never established and partnered my own law offices. I would've never met my wife."

I wiped a tear from my eye. "And I've never been so proud of you."

"I have another surprise for you," he said. "I brought someone to see you."

He rose from the table, looking at his wife. As if on cue, she nodded to him and got to her feet.

"I'm going to use the ladies' room," she said, walking off.

Andy smiled at me as he turned and walked toward the window. He approached a man looking out into the courtyard. I didn't recognize the man by his build or posture. He wore loose-fitted cargo pants and a dark denim jacket. His hair was peppered with gray, cut short, neat. He had something familiar about him, but I wasn't able to place a finger on what it was.

Andy whispered something to him, and he turned around, looking in my direction. I strained to see if I would recognize his face without my glasses. I had left them in my cell. But even if I had brought them, I still would've had a difficult time recognizing the man as a shadow was cast on his face from the positioning of the sunlight through the window.

He was a silhouette in the brilliant stream until he began walking toward me. It was a walk I made out at once. I knew the stroll behind each step he took, and I stood to my feet, my eyes watering and heart racing, as I placed my hands over my mouth.

It was Steve Mitchell.

He still had his youthful face, but bearded, and he wore glasses with a cheery smile I had come to miss through the years.

"Hey, Anne," he said, with a spirited tone, his nonchalant greeting catching me off guard. I hadn't seen him in over thirty years, and the way he welcomed me was as if we'd seen each other last week.

I shook my head, happy to see him. I extended my arms and reached out to hug him.

He came into my arms grinning. I embraced him as tight as I could, squeezing out tears from my eyes. I rested my head on his shoulder, then looked up at him, unable to let go of him.

"Is this allowed?" he asked, half joking.

He had no idea how much I missed him. How I missed the smell of the Old Spice cologne he used to splash all over his clothes and face.

I smelled him, hoping to inhale a trace of the cologne, but he had on something different—a scent I wasn't familiar with.

After a moment, I let go of him, looking into his eyes. He stared back into mine. I smiled, grabbing him by his suit jacket. "Where the hell have you been?" I snapped.

"I'm sorry," he said. "I really am. I tried to come see you after you got arrested. I really did, but they arrested me, too."

I let go of his jacket and hugged him again. "What happened to you?" I asked, my tone soft, passionate.

"The police caught me, and I went to jail, and I wet my pants, and I cried like a two-year-old when they put me behind bars. It was a pitiful sight to see. "

"I'm not talking about that," I said. "What happened to you? Why did it take you so long to come see me?"

"After my parents bailed me out, they put me on punishment. I couldn't leave the basement after school for weeks. Then they sent me away to a college in Oregon. I wasn't allowed to come home—not even on holidays or summer breaks."

I looked at him shaking my head. He shrugged, realizing how pitiful his excuse sounded. But it was the truth. Steve was a mama's boy. He still was.

"You've aged," I said with a smile, folding my arms.

"I finally get to see how the granny you looks," he shot back, joking.

"You've aged well," I said, admiring his handsome features.

"Technically, you should be like ninety now, right?"

I laughed. "Technically."

He sighed, looking at me, his tone softening. "I came looking for you after I graduated from college and moved back home. But you had been moved to another prison. I tried to find your brother, but your family had moved away. No one knew where they went. I was forced to join the Navy by my parents. I did three years overseas, then three more years in Virginia. I almost got married twice, but it never worked out. So, here I am. No wife, no kids, all these years later."

"How did you find me?" I asked him.

"I didn't," he replied. "I gave up looking. Your brother found me. About six weeks ago. He wanted to wait until you received your pardon before bringing me here to see you."

"Well, I'm glad to see you. I never stopped thinking about you. I was always worried about what happened to you."

"I survived," he said. "They dismissed the charges against me. My parents hired a good lawyer. I ended up doing some community service and being an usher in a local church before going off to college. Then came the Navy."

I returned to my seat. "What are you doing for yourself now?"

Steve sat across from me, holding his hands together on the table. "I ended up becoming a YouTube star. I started my own live stream for gaming. I design online video games, as well. Tech stuff. Or, geek stuff, really, but I love it. I spend sixteen hours a day in front of a computer."

"I could've seen that in your future," I laughed.

"You were right about a lot of things in the future," he said. "The GPS and cell phones. If I would've had you around, I might've ended up rich."

"You still can be," I smiled.

He lowered his head. When he looked up at me again, I saw a sudden somberness etched into his expression.

"I missed you, Anne," he said. "I missed you a lot."

"I missed you, too, Steve."

He grinned, sliding down in his chair a bit, as if his toes curled from embarrassment. He cleared his throat and coughed. "So, uh, what now?"

I slightly shook my head, confused. "What do you mean?"

"What are you going to do? You know, like, when you get out of here?"

"I don't know."

He looked around, leaned over the table, getting closer so know one would hear him. "He's still out there, you know."

I nodded, sighing, "I know."

"You can find him. You can still go back and keep any of this from happening. You can stop your mom from meeting Elroy Leonard. You can save her. You can save yourself. Keep yourself from ending up in prison. You can change everything."

I looked down at my aging hands, shaking my head no.

"Why not?" he asked.

"I don't have the nightmares anymore," I said to him. "Like I did before going back in time. I'm the one who got to kill Elroy Leonard this time. I'm at peace with that."

Steve's eyes rolled around as he let out a heavy breath. He didn't want to accept my passive attitude. "Outside of Elroy Leonard, what good came out of this for you?"

I looked up at him and smiled. "I got to meet you, didn't I?"

He smiled. "Yeah, you did."

"We weren't friends in the other timeline. I barely spoke to you. I barely noticed you. I looked down at you—thought you were just some geeky guy pampered by his parents. That's changed. You saved my life, Steve. You became the one thing I never really had after my mother's murder. You became my closest friend."

"You helped me in many ways, too, Anne," he said. "But you still ended up in here, and that's been hard for me to live with. You should still find Singh… *go back*."

I looked up, shifting my gaze toward Andy as his wife appeared, walking toward him, hugging him.

"Listen, I know things got messed up in the original timeline for you," Steve said. "You weren't able to save your mom. But you can do it all over again. Make it better. Isn't that worth the risk? Don't you want to change things?"

I didn't remove my eyes from Andy and his wife. I watched them as they smiled together, held each other close, and I knew their happiness, his happiness, was enough for me.

Without looking at Steve, I whispered my response:

"I wouldn't change a thing."

Made in the USA
Middletown, DE
06 January 2020